I0638458

Young, Black, Talented & Alone

Chapter 1: The First Love

Relationships from a Male point of view

NATHAN ALEXANDER

Young, Black, Talented, and Alone
Copyright @ 2020 by Nathan Alexander

All rights reserved. No parts of this work may be reproduced or transmitted in any form or by any means, electronic or mechanical, including photocopying, or by any information storage or retrieval system, excerpt as it expressly is permitted by the Copyright Act or in writing from Nathan Alexander.

Disclaimer
The information published in this book represents the opinions, personal research, and business experience of the author. Since the success of anyone depends upon the skills and abilities of the person, the author makes no guarantees, and disclaims any personal loss or liabilities that may occur as a result of the use of the information contained herein.

This publication is designed to provide accurate and authoritative information in regard to the subject matter covered in it. It is provided with the understanding that the publisher is not engaged in rendering legal, accounting, or other professional services. If legal advice or other expert assistance is required, the services of a competent professional person should be sought.

ISBN-13: 978-0-578-23270-6

Table of Contents

IV. INTRODUCTION: WHY?

Hey Everyone.

This book sprang from pain and an attempt to gain closure. Like many of my brothers of many colors, I had gone on faith and poured my heart into relationships, hoping for positive outcomes. Along the way, there were good experiences, bad experiences, and those situations that made me ask, "Just what the hell am I supposed to learn from this shit?" And like many out there, I had my heart broken several times, with the first time being the deepest. However, with each experience, you learn exactly what you want (or don't want) in the next relationships and use that wisdom as your learning tools in searching for the next. Believe me, I had a lot to learn. In doing so, I found that in time, you will get over things, and the things that mattered in one relationship had little to no value in another.

I wanted to share my experiences, because I know that I wasn't the only one going through these things. For the other guys out there, the experiences may have been way worse. Each person and relationship is different according to the people, but all remain the same. And that's why I feel that EVERY man goes through that first love (the deepest impact), that trophy girl (who you THINK you may want, but as time goes on, how superficial and shallow that person reveals themselves to be), that work relationship (all good, until you realize that work and play either don't or can't mix), and that physical relationship (outside of puttin' that thang on me, the only thing we seem to have in common is very little to nothin' at all). So yeah, it was that pain, along with wanting to see closure that inspired me to write this.

To the ladies: yes, guys hurt. Guys cry. Guys hang by the phone too, waiting for you to call back and saying that you wanna get back with us. But you'd never know it, unless we confessed it to you. So to that, I present four different books with my personal stories. I hope that these stories give insight for you ladies, and by reading it, hope that you understand our joys, worries, and angst when it comes to taking that leap of faith and first asking you out, followed by trying to build a relationship, only to have things go south, and trying to find closure. I read about it all the time by female authors, but this here is a FIRST, because in written or typed words, you can see for the first time how men feel about the same thing you go through. It's definitely a two-way street, and so I hope that you read with an open mind and form some sort of understanding, along with some head nodding and asking, "Was that me?" It's possible. Anything is possible. Read on for yourself and determine which one of these you were or are.

And to the fellas...hang on and stay strong. Never, ever give up. To put it simply, keep dating until you find that right one. That one who'll put up with your crazy the same way you'll put up with hers. It's a gamble, but hey, if you keep rolling the dice and come up Seven after a while and not crap out, then you just might have a winner on your hands!

So for all my brothers of different colors and other mothers, this one's 4 U.

-Al

Soma,
AKA: The First Love...

Smitten While Sittin'

In nature, the male that is the most colorful, or strongest, or most aggressive is the one that gets the best pick for the female of his choice. Human nature is by no means any different. However, for human males that show no athletic ability or dress style, these are the ones that have to come up with other schemes in order to make up for what they don't have and get what they want.

Such was the case with Soma. We met during my 11th grade year at one of the local high school talent shows, when there were just friendly rivalries between schools, and there was very little violence going on. So that meant that if you dug somebody at a rival school, you could go up there and not have to take a lot of shit from anybody. At any rate, when I met ol' girl, I was impressed.

Soma was tight. She looked as if she was Puerto Rican or something other than a sista. She was about five foot four, light-skinned, hairy, with beautiful teeth, and big, beautiful bouffant hair. We were in the eighties, so please understand what was hot in fashion and styles for women. Big hair was the thing for girls, and for the light-skinned brothas, it was definitely our decade. Shoot, Prince had just come out with Purple Rain, and he had the chicks swooning, so everybody on the light tip was trying to look like him. I fell into that category. I was wiry, but I had on a black trench coat, some tight-ass jeans, and a white button-down. I didn't have a perm like that brotha (Momma just wasn't gon' let me do it), but I did have hella Vaseline in my hair for that slicked-down, Alexander O'Neal look, as well as eyeliner (Hey, Prince was my idol).

Anyway, I was dressed like that when I went to the talent show. I came struttin' in, lookin' all around, convinced that ALL the women wanted me. I was so blind, so naïve. I saw my boy, Karl, up in the bleachers, chillin'. Karl was kinda smooth. He was light-skinned, tall and gangly, and also had what Black folks would call a 'good grade' of hair. He wore designer clothes, and had a car, so brotha was popular. Me, I got to the show on public transportation. No way was I drivin', according to my dad. So it was either try to get a ride daily, or public transportation, or the cheese, a.k.a. the school bus. Forget that. Public transportation all the way.

So there Karl was, up in the bleachers with a couple of honeys. I made it up the stairs despite the laughs (I was used to it), and sat down next to him.
"What's up, man?" I asked. The girls that were sitting next to him were laughing at first, then when they saw me, they stopped. And then laughed some more. At me. One of 'em that was laughing I noticed was cute as hell. Our eyes met for a moment, and then she looked away in shyness.

"What's up, Al?" We slapped hands. "Good to see ya."
"Yeah, glad to make it. You know how public transportation is and shit."
"Nah, don't know. I drive." In addition to being popular, Karl could also be a dick.
"Riiight. So who're your friends?" I asked.

"This here's Natalie. And this one's Soma."

"Hi ladies. My name's Al."

"Hi Al." Again my eyes were on Soma. "And how YOU doin'?" I asked, givin' her the sexy look, courtesy of Prince.

"Fine." "I see that." She blushed. Smiled and blushed. I think I kinda had her then.

"Can I sit here with you, then?" I asked, stroking my Vasellenic hair. Greasier than a mu'fucka.

"Sure."

"Well, okay I won't. I'll just sit right...wait, what did you say?"

"I said 'sure'. It's okay. You can sit with me."

Natalie was like, "Girl, no, don't do that! Look at him! Shit, at least think about yo' reputation!"

"Natalie, relax. He's okay."

"Yeah, Natalie, relax. I'm o.k." I hopped up to where she was sitting, and we enjoyed the show together. I had the chance to really look at her, study her. She definitely looked exotic, like a mixed-breed. It was the spring, and it was hot, so she had on a little camisole, with her breasts pushing out, and some tight jeans. She definitely was sexy. And she smelled good as well. All I could picture her in was nothing, just laying on a bed in some exotic position, all oiled up and shit, and I was right there with her.

Karl had his arm around Natalie, and she was leaning in towards him, her head on his arm. He looked over at me and grinned. Then he motioned for me to try my luck. Shiiit, I was in a public place and was already bein' laughed at. I could take that. But to try that shit would be suicide, and I don't do rejection well. Besides, I was just getting to know her. So instead of doing that bullshit, I leaned over during one of the acts that was terrible, and whispered in her ear, "The show's kinda cool, huh?"

"Yeah, pretty cool." That's all she said. I wanted to talk more, but I don't think she did. When the show was over, I asked Karl for a ride, which he did with hella attitude. But before I left…I gave Soma some more Prince sexy gaze, along with a little more conversation.

"Well…" I spoke slowly, "I really had a good time tonight."

"I did too."

"And meeting you tonight made my good time even better."

"Oh."

"So maybe we could, you know…" Karl cut me off.

"Hey man, let's go if you want a ride. Drop your ass at Hightower, and you'll have to make it on from there, since you wanna take your time an' shit. Let's go! Soma don't wanna hear no lame-ass wanna get together begging speech from you! 'Sides, I think she already got a man!"

I looked at Soma. "That true?"

"Nah," she said. "Karl's just a dick." Damn, we both had something in common!

I laughed. "Damn. We must be thinking on the same level, 'cuz that's EXACTLY what I was thinking.

"SOMA!" Natalie called out. "Our ride's here! Let's go!"

"Yeah, Al! And your ride ain't gon' wait all damn night, either. So get the molasses out'cha ass and let's go!" Damn, Karl was such a...well you know.

"Gotta go. Nice meeting you though."

"Same here," I said. Karl grabbed Natalie and gave her a goodnight kiss. Shoot, I wanted one too. But that was later. The girls headed out the door, and Karl and I got the hell on as well. Riding home, Karl joned and talked about me like a dog. But I didn't care, 'cuz I saw who was gonna be my woman. And this is the truth: I felt it. And when you feel something like that, it can't be wrong, right?

Right?

The weekend came and went. All I could think about was her: How cute, how fine. And she wasn't even tryin'. I like that kind of woman; the kind that ain't gotta put on airs and just naturally pretty, both inside and out. Soma was definitely that. First of all, she had been kind to me where so many others made fun of me. Like her friend, whom I thought was a saditty bitch. I don't think it was pity, I think that she was just being genuinely nice.

Secondly, our eyes met, and SHE shied away. Usually it's me. At that time at sixteen years old, women intimidated me. But not her. With her, I felt so comfortable, and I didn't even know her. Since Karl knew her, I think that she must have either grown up with him or she stayed in his neighborhood. At any rate,

I wanted to take a chance with this, see where it might go, so I did the ol' skool thang, and composed a note. In it, I talked about how I felt when I first met her, when our eyes met, and how I felt that in those moments at the show that there might have been a connection. I wrote and said that if she didn't have a boyfriend, then would she seriously think about giving me a chance and go on a date with me? I ended it by saying that I understood if she had one, but nothing was, is, and never will be permanent. And I also included my number. I figured I had a chance if she read it to the end and discovered that I was asking her to call. Now all I had to do was to convince Karl to take his ass over there (since he drove) and give it to her.

Monday came, but I didn't have the nerve. I had to work my way up to that shit. Like I said, I am NOT a fan of rejection, and at that point, I couldn't take no for an answer. Tuesday and Wednesday came, but I still wasn't ready. Instead I waited for Thursday to come, and that my friends, was the day.

Karl and I were both sitting in drafting class. Bullshit class where the teacher was crazy and you took the class only if you thought about becoming an engineer. The only reason I was in this class was because of my momma, who had "high hopes" for me. Hell, I had high hopes, too, but it wasn't to become no damn engineer. So I sucked. Don't get me wrong…I could draw, but I ain't used no instruments to draw those damn things in the book to scale!

So today, instead of the usual horsing around in class, I was in a serious mode. Brotha was on a mission.

So while Mr. Allen was running his mouth, I tapped Karl. We were both sitting in the back of the class, so I know if we weren't payin' attention, he wasn't payin' attention to us. Guess he knew he was gonna fail a brotha anyway.

"Karl?" I whispered.

"What?"

"Can I ask you somethin'?"

"Naw."

I ignored his ignorant comment. "Those girls that you were sitting with at the talent show. Who were they again?"

"Uhhh...let's see," he said rubbin' his chin. "Got so many."

"Brotha, please. Your girl's friend. What was her name?"

"Oh. You talkin' 'bout Soma! What about her?"

"Hell yeah...Soma! That's right? How you know her?" The bell rang. End of class, and we could use our adult voices now. We walked on out into the hallway.

"Now," I said. "Soma. How you know her?"

"How I know her? She lives around the corner from me in the hood, y'know?"

"Yeah. Why you wanna know?"

"I'm uh...just askin'."

"Yeah, right. You must wanna holla at her or somethin'."

"Could be." I looked down. " What can you tell me about her?"

"She a cool girl. I tried to get in them draws, but she ain't wanna do nothin'. Other than that, she cool."

"You think she was feelin' me at the show?"

"Yeah, she looked like she was interested. And she ain't no fake, y'know?"

"Okay. Yeah. Well look here," I pulled the letter out of my bookbag. Shit was folded up all nice and neat and even stapled. "I want you to ride over to her house and give her this." He took the note from me, and stared.

"You got some ride money?" he asked.

"Ride money? What for?"

To put gas in my ride to go over there and drop your message off! Hell you think I ride on...fumes?"

"Dang, brotha, here..." Now I didn't have Job One, but I managed to give him three dollars, and he just stared at me.

"What?"

"Three dollars?!"

"I'll hook you up next week."

"Three dollars?!"

"Now you know good and damn well I ain't got no jo—"

"Three dollars?!"

"Shuddup, it's all I got!"

"Three..." Before he could even get it out again, I popped him in the chest.

"Just do it, okay?" He rubbed his chest and just stared.

"You ain't havta hit me."

"Well, I'm sorry, but you just kept on bitchin' about three dollars and I just don't wanna hear no more about it." He took the money, though. "I ain't doin' this shit no more for your ass!"

"Yeah you will. You will. As long as I've got gas money for you, you'll be there."

The bell rang and it was on. I decided to try and impress her by doing what I knew how to do best, and that was by drawing.

I started dreaming up images. What could I say about the situation and how could I best express that I wanted to get with her? *Al likes Soma. Hi! I see you.* Nah, that was *too* lame. I like what I see…nah. *Al is crazy for Soma.* Hmmm, like that one, just let me innovate. *Al is crazy 4 Soma.* Yeah, that's it! So now that I had my idea down pat, I started sketching. The next day, I saw Karl in class. Interrogation was in effect.

"What's up, man?"

"What's up?"

" You know what's up! Didja tell her for me?"

"Yeah, after I went by there twice."

"I mean, did you actually see her, or did you leave her a note?" I whispered.

"Yeah, I left her a note."

"What?" I couldn't believe this fool!

He shifted his paper. I edged closer to his desk. "Naw brotha, I saw her and talked to her."

"So what did she say?"

"Well…she said that she ain't got no man, but she barely remembers you."

"What?" I said to myself. But we practically vibed that night. How could she not have remembered me? I was truly in a state of shock after that. So then I said, "Well listen, I want you to do one more thing for me, and then I'll take it from there." Heavy sigh on his part.

Then "What is it now?"

"About a week from today, I want you to give her this thing I'm working on."

Then he got loud. "Damn man, why can't you deliver…"

"Mr. Alexander!" my teacher yelled out. "Sorry." I reached out and grabbed Karl by the arm. "Look man, I told you, how in the hell can I give her this when I'm on the bus? How?"

"Leggo of me!" He snatched away. "How you say? Tell yo momma to give your ass 90 cents to ride Marta and do it your damn self then!"

"Hey Karl! I'm asking you to do this as a friend! Plus I'm *giving* you gas money so you can take this over there, which ain't a far distance from where you live, 'cuz I know you'll probably be ridin' some of your broads around."

"So what'cha sayin'?"

"What I'm sayin' is, do this shit for me, and stop actin' like a bitch!" He shut up then. Then quietly, he was like, "A'ight then," and proceeded to shut up. I went and crept a sheet of large paper from art class, took it home, and began to work on the project, starting Saturday.

Ya'll, the funny things we do for love, especially in high school when it's lust first, 'cuz our hormones are working overtime at that age (rather nagging), and we know it, especially with the fellaz. We will screw anything that moves, *anything* with a hole in it. At first I was thinkin' that, especially being my height (I was only 5'2" at the time), and the fact that I had never had a girlfriend during my entire high school career. It ain't like I didn't try. Things just went bad whenever I did make the effort. Well, I felt that things were about to change, and for the better. Man, I must've missed a whole week of assignments to complete (I was a nerd, too) this piece of work to give to Soma. But I considered it to be my high school masterpiece. Al iz Crazy 4 Soma in graffitti. Draw, erase, draw, erase. Finish it in pencil, now outline in black. Color. Color. More color. Damn, too much color. Oh well, shit's tight anyway. She probably couldn't tell the difference.

On Monday, I gave it to Karl. It was a huge 20 x 32 fucking billboard, folded into a clasp envelope designed to enclose standard 8 x 11 documents. That, and a letter letting her know just how much I wanted to meet with her again, and how I couldn't get her off of my mind ever since I saw her (and ya'll, I really couldn't). I also told her that I felt that she was my soulmate (the first of five other women whom I also felt were my soulmates later on in life), and lastly included my phone number for her to call. Now I'm a patient person, but do you know that it took this heifer almost two weeks to call me from the time that her mail was delivered to her from Karl? Oh yeah, I was pissed. Then finally, one night she hit me up and we were good from there. Conversation went like this:

"Hello?"

"Al?"

"Yeah, who's this?"

"This is Soma."

Pause on my part. My heart started beating fast as hell. It was so exciting!! But I had to play it cool.

"Oh hey. Wassup Shawty? Yo! Look here, I've been trying to…"

I caught myself just then and started over. Be cool, Al.

"I mean um…so what's up, girl?"

"Nada. I got your picture from Karl, and I gotta say I like. It's really nice. Who taught you how to draw like this?"

Proudly, I answered, "Nobody. I taught myself." She got really excited then.

"That's good! Like I said, it's really nice. Me likey."

"Oh, okay. 'Preciate it." She liked it! Yeah!

"There's only one problem, though." Problem? What the hell was she talkin' about?

"Oh yeah?" I said. "What's that?"

"I'm not trying to be funny or anything like that, but…I really…don't…remember who…you…are."

Pause on my part. Pregnant pause. Pregnant, long-ass pause with disbelief. Was she for real?

"Hello?" she called out.

"Yeah, I'm still here."

"I'm sorry, but I honestly don't."

"You mean to tell me that you don't remember me from when Karl introduced me to you from the talent show?"

"Vaguely." *Well damn, that's kinda cold* I said to myself.

"Did you say something, Al?"

"Naw Shawty!" I decided to dissect the situation. After a moment, "So you really don't remember me, huh?" Wow. Couldn't believe that one.

"No, not really. As I said before, only vaguely. But your drawing is beautiful."

"Well, would you like to meet the artist of this work? Again?"

"Yeah. I mean, I ain't got no problem with it. Are you asking me out?" I started sweating on my palms on the other end. I ain't never had a girl to ask me that.

"Yeah! Uh…is…is that what it sounds like to you? Like I'm asking you out?"

"Sounds like it to me," she said. I decided to get bold then.

"Well dammit, if it sounds that way, then that's what it is!"

"Huh?"

"Yeah! Yeah Soma, I'm asking you out. Even though you don't remember me from the show, with the Prince look and everything. However, the good thing is that you can *get* to know me by going out *with* me. "

"Well, that's cool. I guess I could do that. You don't **sound** dangerous."

"I'm not…but I could be. Only if you wanted me to be, though." I shot back.

"Oooh." Wonder what she was thinking?

Young, Black, Talented, & Alone

I continued. "So it's a date?"

"Sure, Mister Al. When?"

"How about next weekend?"

"Okay. About what time?"

"Uhhh…around eight thirty?" I stammered.

"Make it nine."

"You got it. Oh, I almost forgot…where do you live?" She gave me the address, and then it was *on.* I…had…a…date!! YES!!

The next week was spent begging my dad to let me use his car for next Saturday (the decided date). This was accomplished with a great deal of difficulty, but dammit, it got done. Lemme first explain to you something abut my old man. He had me late in his life, so it's like we're three generations apart in age and tastes. That simply meant that we don't have nothin' in common. That also meant that he's stuck in his ol' school beliefs, which justifies his stubbornness when it comes to trying new things. He's a mean son of a gun, and it's hard to believe that back in the day, he was a trendsetter.

When other people would carry a knife or a razor to cut you with in case somebody started some shit, my dad started the idea of carrying a razor *and* a pistol. That meant that he'd probably get you one way or another if you messed with him.

My older cousins who went fishing with him before I was born told me that if folks provoked him, he was always mumbling, "I'ma go get my pistol or cut they damn ass." Always going to get that damn pistol.

What he probably didn't realize is that by the time he got to his car to get his pistol, whoever he was starting some shit with or vice versa, they woulda shot his ass way before he would've made it to the car. He was just ignorant on that fact, 'cuz he thought he was Superman or some invincible dude. Not.

As said before, we had absolutely nothing in common, so you can imagine what a bitch it was getting me to convince him to use his car. The drama started on Tuesday, and didn't stop until an hour before I was supposed to pick Soma up.

"Whaddya want the car for again?" he growled.
"I wanna use it, 'cuz I got a date."
"With who?"
"This girl named Soma."
"Who the hell's Soma? She new?" I started to get agitated.
"Shoot, she the *only*. Pop, man, what's with all the questions? You gonna let me use the car or what?" He just stared at me. Then, "You old enough to drive yet?" Unreal.
"Okay listen. *You're* the one who took me to get my license in the first place, remember? So why don't you tell me?'

He shifted in his chair. "Ain't no need to get smart, boy." Clearly the old man was going senile, but was clearly trying to hang on. Then out of nowhere, "Why are you in my face, boy? What is it that you want?"

"Pop," I began slowly.
"I...need...the...car...for...a...date."

"What time you goin' to pick her up?"

"Around nine."

"Nine?! Boy, that's way too late for a date to start out!"

"It's not until the weekend, Pop."

Then my mom came in the room and interrupted this discussion with good common sense.

"Alexander," she started, "Why are you givin' this boy the third degree?"

"Aw woman, I was just makin' sure that he doesn't go out and get wild," he snorted. Then he looked at me. "Shit, I ain't no fool. I know how ya'll young boys like to get drunk and then smoke that dope. Get ya'll fools REAL high."

"Pop..."

"Alexander, that was almost twenty years ago," my mom snapped. "This boy don't smoke no dope, do you Al?" Always in my corner, that's what I'm talkin' about.

"No, Ma." My dad decided to finish what he started. He didn't care.

"He better not...else I'll havta go get my pistol."

I shook my head. "Okay, so anyway, Pop...you gon' let me use the car? I'm tired of playin' this game with you."

"Can you or may you?" Damn!! Ya'll see what I mean now? A lot of bullshit for nothin'! My mom just went into their bedroom and came back with her keys.

"Here Al, take my car. I don't know why yo' daddy is giving you such a hard time, but here. What time you gonna be back?"

"About twelve or one." I had my hand out, but she didn't give 'em up.

"What? What's wrong?" I asked.

"Just a minute, Al. I ain't gonna give you a lecture, but I am gonna say this: Ain't nothin' in the streets for you after one in the morning, except trouble. Your best bet is to be in here by one. That way, the girl's daddy won't be worried about what time he's gonna see his daughter, and your daddy won't be worried if you're out there smokin' that dope or if ya'll got a hotel, or doin' whatever."

"I hear ya. Thank you Ma." I took the keys and was walking to the door. As I walked out, I could hear my dad talkin' trash. "Why didn't he wanna take my car?" "Aw shut up, Alexander!" I heard my momma say. Enough of that, I was out.

Winning!

That first date was off the hook. Off the hook, I tell ya! I pulled up exactly at nine. All the while I was wondering what in the hell we were gonna do. Both of us were underage to really do anything considered fun. However, when I got to the door, both of her parents were standing with her. That was interesting, I thought. I got out the car and walked up the driveway.

"Hi, Al, these are my parents."

"Hello." I held out my hand to shake her dad's hand, but he just stared at me. Okay.

"They just wanted to meet the person who did the artwork for me."

"Really?" I glanced at her parents again. "Did you really like it?" I said to both of them. Her father spoke up. "Fascinating." Then the man pulled it out.

"What the hell does it say?" he said, turning it all around.

"It says 'Al Iz Crazy 4 Soma.'"

"Crazy? As in you wanna try and hurt my daughter?"

"What? No sir, it's not that. It's just that…"

"Son, if you think you're gonna mess my daughter up, I suggest that you go on home right now."

"Daddy!" Soma exclaimed. "He's just messin' with you, Al." She took my hand. "Let's go." We walked down the driveway.

"Nice meeting you sir, ma'am." Do you know that they stood there until we got all the way down and into the car, and *then* they went inside? They were trippin'! But back to Soma.

"So, you remember me now?" Soma was starin' her ass off.

"Yeah! Yeah... I do."

"Well, that's a relief." We drove down the street. "So what are we doin' tonight?" she asked.

"Well, we got one of three options...bowling, the movies, or the dance at my church. Now which one..."

"The dance."

"Well, that was easy. You got it, darlin'." With that, it was on.

We rolled up to my church about ten. That meant that we only had two hours and fifteen minutes left before I had to be back at the crib. We got in there quick as hell, paid our admission, walked through the door, and were surprised that it was PACKED! I couldn't believe it! Then again I could, because of the fact that not being twenty one really limited you on how much fun you could really have, so a lot of people from Doug, Mays, and Therrell were there, since the church was in a central location where all schools had access to. We got on the dance floor, and ya'll know...I had to show the skills. Run D.M.C.'s "It's Like That" was blastin' out of the speakers, and so I served her with the Smurf, the Yeek, the Prep, and the Shabba Doo (those from Atlanta reading this know exactly what I'm talkin' 'bout...HA!!) Oh yeah, the Que Dog, the Tip, and the Mo-Joe were also done. Yeah, ol' Soma brought out the best in me. I could tell she was impressed, 'cuz she was like, "Okay, slow down now...you just can't keep hurtin' these folks like this" with her eyes darting around nervously. Looking back, I think rather than be impressed, she may have been embarrassed, 'cuz I just got buck wild. Especially during that time in the party when (and you know it happens at every Black folks party) the infamous Soul Train line starts to form (the Electric Slide was way unheard of back then, that's for the old folks).

As a matter of fact, I KNOW that she was embarrassed first hand, because when it was my turn to go down the line, she grabbed my arm, telling me, "Hey Al, you don't need to hurt 'em anymore tonight, okay? Trust me on this…" Hmph. Forget that. I was goin'. When I started after this girl before me, I heard Soma say, "Oh God…", and then bury her face in her hands. I did not care or give a DAMN. All I could hear was "Go…go…go…go!" I was rockin' it, ya'll, 'cuz I *knew* I was one of the people there who turned it up and then out. When I got to the end and went back around to her, a very seductive slow jam was on (International Lover , by you know who). She didn't say one word, just took my hand and pulled me up to her bumper, ya'll. As I was dancing close with her, she whispered in my ear, "Please…you've done enough tonight. Just hold me." And being a gentleman, I did what I had to do, just to make her happy. And then…out of the blue, she just kissed me!! Long kiss, too, with tongue and everything!! I may have been a nerd once, but I was reborn! My life was getting better and better by the minute!

Oh yeah, ya'll. Did I forget to tell ya'll that Soma looked good tonight? I mean, she…looked…goot.

REALLY DAMN GOOT. So goot that I had to kiss her again…and then again. What the hell, one more time for good measure, ignoring all the catcalls of "Damn, why don't ya'll get a room?" "How long ya'll gon' be 'fore somebody comes up for air?" "Ay, yo…how's both of ya'll's stomachs taste?" I just stayed silent, brothers were just jealous anyway and hatin'. I just kept looking deep into her eyes, and she knew what time it was.

"You ready to get out of here?" I said.
"Yeah, I am. I really don't like being the center of attention. Let's go."

At that time it was about twelve. I still had thirty minutes before I returned the car, so we bailed.

Back in the eighties, it was cool to leave a party, and either go to the King over by Greenbriar Mall or to the park and make out. Let me define and make this clear: Making out did not, I repeat, did not mean tryin' to bust somebody out in the car, but instead put "passion marks" on somebody's neck so that you could tell that a person got some action over the weekend. However, if you also got some during the make out session, then that was cool, too. We rolled to the park, and I almost got some, had it not been for her breathy moans of "Baby, I gotta go home…please." Damn! It was all good, tough…there was always a next time, sho'nuff.

After that night, I absolutely *knew* that Soma was gonna be my lady. I could just feel it in our conversations during those sleepless nights on the phone. And during those convos, it was about two months before the topic of sex came up. Now I'm sure that since we had gone out and had been talkin' for a minute, it had been on our brains all of this time, but we never spoke it into existence. That is until now, goin' into the third month. One night, we talked about it from the time it was brought up 'til the wee hours of the morning, when we both had to get up for school. In the conversation, we mapped it all out. We planned to do it one weekend at her house while her parents were there and sleeping. See, she had a split level, so at one o'clock in the morning, her parents were either going to be confined to their bedroom doing things, or they were going to be knocked tha fuck out. Why did we choose when her parents were there? Shit, why not? Made things more exciting and made us both want to see if we could get away with it. The first thing I needed was transportation. I had this friend named Marc, who had a ten speed bike. Since I couldn't use the car on a regular basis, and Marc lived around the way, I got with him on using the bike, and told him everything. I gotta tell you, when I first told him, he was like, "Dag, man (the first brotha I knew that didn't curse at all), she must be somethin' else if you wanna get it that bad."

"Yeah! That and I really dig her. As a matter of fact, she could be the one. She could actually be Mizzus Alexander."

"Dang!!! Okay, I hear ya! Just be careful. You wouldn't wanna get in somethin' you couldn't get out of." "Don't worry about me. You just get that bike and let me worry about the rest. I'll bring your bike back in time." "You'd better."
"Whatever. Transportation? Checck."

I Just Wanna Love Ya…ATL Style

The night of the Great Sexcapade had finally arrived. I waited until my folks were knocked out and then made my escape under the garage door by lifting it slightly. My folks slept on the top level, and I lived in the basement, so the only problem I had to worry about was the back gate making a noise as it swung open. Oh, and the dog barking. I know some of ya'll may be asking yourselves, "How come you just didn't go through the front door?" Well, my folks crushed that two years prior to me getting with Soma by installing a burglar alarm equipped with an inside motion sensor attached to the door. So when the door opened, the alarm always went off like a pager, so I couldn't do nothin' with that. The garage was easier to use.

I left a note in my room, so in case they came down, I thought I would have an alibi saying that I had gone jogging. Seventeen year old thinking, ya'll. Just plain stupid. And horny. Lifted the garage door, petted the dog, climbed over the fence, and made my way to Marc's house. I was a little paranoid being out there walking, but the booty was calling.

The plan was going, well, according to plan. Marc didn't have a dog, just this senile bat of a grandmother who called everybody an "ol' butthole." So I had to watch out for this bat, 'cuz she was up at all times of the night, and always got out the house and roamed all areas of his folks' back yard and sometimes the front. He was supposed to meet me in the yard, but he didn't. Instead, the bike was out there with a note attached to it, saying 'Bring it back'. Didn't I tell him I would? Damn. I took the note off and started pedaling.

You know, when you're ridin' a bike at twelve-twenty in the morning, you get to see things you wouldn't normally see in the day, and at early parts of the night. I know I did. From hookers to bums jumping out, doin' the wave, talkin' 'bout some damn "Heyyy man!" and beggin' for money, to the dope boys, to brothas that just ain't got nothin' else to do but cruise and walk the streets, I saw it all. I know I was rolling, and flew by all of these things, not because I didn't have any money, but mainly 'cuz I was scared as hell. You would be too, at a little past midnight, seventeen years old, and on a damn bike. I didn't stop for shit. I pedaled on and on 'til finally I came up on the house. Before I came over, we agreed that I would need a signal in order to let her know that I was out there. My dumb ass settled on an owl call. I came around the back of the house, and put the bike behind the toolshed. It was about twelve –forty. Brotha man was sweatin'. I went to Soma's window.

"Who!" I called out. Nobody came to the window or to the sliding glass door that I was now standing in front of.

"Who!" Again no response. Damn, did this girl fall asleep? She must've thought I was joking when I said I was coming. A little louder and a little longer.

"Whooooo!!" The light came on in her room, finally. And so did her parents'. I jumped like a runaway slave with the dogs after him behind the toolshed. Her daddy opened up their window and stuck his head out.

Young, Black, Talented, & Alone

"What the hell is goin' on? Hello!" he called out. He closed the window and called out "Soma!" I guess the windows weren't insulated. 'cuz I could hear the conversation.

"Yes, Daddy?"

"You hear somethin'?"

"No Daddy."

"Then why are you up?" Pause. I was sweatin, tryin' to anticipate what lie she was gonna come up with. Then there it was.

"Why am I up? Why am *I* up? 'Cuz you yelled over here and to ask me if I heard something!"

"Well, did you hear anything? Like an owl? I didn't even know we had owls in Atlanta."

"No, Daddy."

"You sure?"

"Positive. Go back to bed and stop screaming."

"All right. Good night, honey."

"Good night." He stuck his big head back in the window, and in a matter of minutes, his lights were back out. Hers stayed on as she kept peering into the darkness. Finally she lifted the window.

"Al?" she called out in a low voice. I appeared before her.

"Soooma, what's up, girl?" I was smiling. She smiled right back.

"Nothin'. I'll be right down."

A few seconds later (which seemed like an eternity when you're sneakin around), she was at the back of the house opening up the sliding glass door.

"Come on in," she whispered. I tiptoed in and we went right upstairs and into her room. When we got up there, we're just sittin' on the bed, still smilin'.

"Dag, girl. You thought I wasn't comin'?" I asked, looking around the room.

"I fell asleep. Sorry."

"Hey, don't worry about it. I thought I wasn't coming myself." She laughed. She had a sense of humor. That was good.

"So," I started, "Where's your drawing?"

She pointed over to the side of her bed. "It's still in the envelope." What the…?

"Still in the envelope? Why you ain't put it up yet?"

"In time, my good friend. In time." I felt insulted. "What'sa matter with it?" I asked. "You ashamed of it?"

"Course not," she said. "I think it's one of the most original and beautiful pieces of work I've ever seen. I just want you to get in good with my parents first. Then I'll put it up. It's like a tradition for me. After a boy gets in good with my folks, *then* I feel comfortable displaying or wearing things that they give me. No offense."

"None taken." By that time, I went to the next step and lay down, feet stretched towards the headboard. She stood up. Damn, Soma was looking good. She had on this blue sports tank top, and some gray jogging shorts. I'm a foot man sometimes, so I was checking out her feet. They were pretty. Then she took her bra off. Then the sweatpants. I looked her all over. Good Lawd, she was fine as hell, and I was as about as hot as a pot of boiling water with some ramen noodles in it.

"You like what you see?" she asked. Hell yeah, I liked it! All in my face, what's not to like?

"Come here." That was all I could say at that time. She came over and sat next to me.

"What's up?"

"You know. Hold on a second." I stood up and started taking off my clothes, except for the draws. That would come later. When I finished, I lay back down on the bed, but she was still sitting on the edge of the bed, like she was scared or something.

"Come here," I whispered again. She leaned over to me.

"Why I gotta come to you? This is my room!"

"Cuz I said so. We can talk about the first thing that comes up, a'ight?'

"'Kay."

She finally lay down on me, then straightened up with a smile.

"What's wrong, baby?"

"Got a rock down there, don'cha?"

"All for you, baby girl. All for YOU! Come on, let's get with the gittin'!" She hesitated.

"You got what we need?"

"Right here, Ms. S." I reached down and picked up my jeans. "Reach in here." She pulled out about fifteen of those mugs. "Why you got so many? What did you expect us to be doin'?"

"You can never have too many, girl." She reached down and touched my boy again. Gripped it. "Mmm. I guess you're right. Hurry up."

She didn't have to ask me twice. Forty two seconds later…and that was just the first time. Had to get warmed up. And then it was on…

I won't go into any more detail, but let's just say that we were a perfect fit together. Three times that night. Cowgirl. Reverse cowgirl. Missionary. Doggystyle. Sideways. Sixty-ninein', we did it ALL. After all that friction and gymnastics, we both fell asleep after that third time, and then woke up to her mom and dad foolin' around. I knew it was time to go when I heard her mom go, "Not in the ear, baby, not tonight…but…right…there…yeah, that's it, Daddy" was all I could hear her mom say. I was trippin'. I was like, "Oh My God!" Just in time to hear her mother moan "Oh My God!" as well. Yeah, time to go. Silently we made our way down the stairs, and back to the sliding glass door. We still heard them from downstairs, and it was getting louder. I really had to go after that. I gave her a Frenchie, ending with "I'll see you later." Soma looked at me starstruck.

"'Kay."
"Will I see you later?"

"You sure will. Just go before they decide to come out the room." I slid out the door, went back 'round the toolshed, and got Marc's bike. I was out.

Ahhh, Southern love. Ain't nothin' else in the world quite like it. It was a good night.

That night was the beginning of a wonderful three year relationship. From that point (after I got in good with her parents), it was me and Soma going everywhere and doing everything together. Me and Soma here, me and Soma there, me and Soma at all the parties, Bar-B-Ques, Six Flags, every damn where. We hung so tight that first year, that all of our friends and people who didn't know of us but who had heard of us swore up and down that our next step was gonna be marriage straight outta high school. I didn't know about that, but I did agree that everything was going well…almost too well.

On my parent's side, my mom liked her, my dad liked her, hell, my whole family adored her. Church, dinner, movies, Piedmont Park on Sundays, riding Marta just to be riding, visiting my relatives, hanging out with her family, we were always together. I remember that I had invited her to church one time to hear me bust out a solo. At first, I thought that she wasn't coming, 'cuz I didn't see her as it got closer for me to perform. Then they called out all visitors to come up to the altar and get a flower. And there she was, coming to the altar, looking up at me in the choir pew, just grinnin' like a Cheshire cat in all her glory. That inspired me, and I did my solo. Later on, my Mom would say that I sang loud and all out of tune 'cuz she was there, and it was like I had to prove something. Life was wonderful, couldn't ask for more. Then that third year came.

Jedi Mind Tricks

Third year with Soma started out pretty good. I managed to complete the last of my classes as a Senior, and graduated from Douglass, got admitted to Morehouse in the fall, and was determined to make a name for myself. However, Freshman Year didn't quite start out the way I expected it to. At Morehouse, I made a name for myself all right. It was when I got called out from our first assembly over in Sale Hall during Freshman Week. I showed up late, and one of the sayings at the House is "to be early is to be on time, and to be on time is late." I showed up only ten minutes...ten minutes ya'll after the session was in progression.

Man, as soon as I hit the door, they brought me on stage. I thought that I had stood out with something that I had done. I thought I was special, until I saw four other brothas being brought on stage as well. I didn't think nothing of it... until I was made an example of because I was late. The upperclassmen acted like some bitches. So after that incident, I would make sure that they would never chastise me again.

I started making a name for myself by entering the Freshman Talent Show as a "street dancer," not one of those Gene Anthony Ray boys from the movie Fame. I wasn't gon' do no ballet, or no damn interpretive dances of my life's journey til now. And I damn sure wasn't gonna wear no tights and do splits or a tumbling act all over the floor. Not gonna happen. Instead, I had another partna who graduated with me, and we got together with that Atlanta style dancing. and turned that show out. Folks at Morehouse and Spelman had never seen anything like that, so we were a hit. So much that the upperclassmen guys startin' hating after that, 'cuz we made lots of female friends, all of them asking us to dance for them (in more ways than one). I made especially good friends with this one girl from Michigan named Torion. Did I tell Soma about Torion, and vice versa? I'll let ya'll figure that one out. No, wait…I'll tell ya'll.

So me and my boy (and a couple of other guys that we had recruited) were getting ready to dance at Clark Atlanta University in the AUC campus wide talent show. I had invited Soma, but Torion said she might be coming too. I figured that was cool, because I knew with that crowd (by now our dance crew was way popular with all four campuses) that there was no way in hell that Soma would see or know who Torion was in that theater. Wrong. When we came out on stage, guess who it was sitting right next to each other in the damned front row? Needless to say, I was nervous, because in tryin' to get some play from T, I told her that Soma was my ex. We were jammin', but I kept my eye on both of 'em, and sure enough, Torion started runnin' her mouth to Soma, just tryin' to dig up dirt!! All through the dance, I saw Soma's face go through a bunch of emotions: from disbelief to anger, then from hurt to betrayal. Before we even finished, Torion got up and walked …correction, STORMED out, leaving Soma there with tears running down her face. After that, all I heard for a week was "Don't talk to me" from Soma.

I kept trying to call her, and the phone would just ring and ring. This shit went on for a week until she finally decided to answer. Guess she was still pissed.

"Can I come by?" I'd ask, like nothing happened.

"Nope. Busy." (click) Karma is a muthafucka. I tried a couple more times to reach her but she didn't wanna hear it. And just 'cuz of that, I could feel the relationship starting to cool down. I didn't know she was jealous like that. Never showed it, never expressed it. I guess that the show was the trigger, because she probably didn't think that I was in college and try to get with other girls, even though she had one more year in high school and thought that she was still my boo.

After that incident, us as a couple started to unravel even more. Her mom worked at Spelman, and now she started to come up there an awful lot. I think because of the incident she started becoming very insecure with me being across the street and also becoming a campus celebrity because of the group. Added to this was the fact that me and my boy had started giving dance lessons to women across the AUC, and you know what could happen after that. I started getting a lot more numbers and a lot more play. This didn't help our relationship at all. On Soma's end, paranoia, suspicion, mistrust, arguments, irrationality in thinking, and finally just plain ol' "Are you screwing any other women?" had consumed her. It was always a big-ass argument that always led to the question below.

"Well are you?"

"Naw, girl!"

"Yeah right."

"Soma, I ain't gotta prove nothing to you. My word is bond. I ain't fucking nobody else."

"Whatever, Al."

"Yeah…whatever."

In time, these slick little responses turned serious. So serious that when I called her one time, she went ahead and made a decision. On that day, it was the same old accusations, until she was like, "Fuck it. You know what? I think we need to give each other some space…you know, take it easy until we figure out what we really want."

It caught me off guard. Way off guard. I was like, "What the hell for? I already know what I want."

"Do you? Do you really know?"

"Yeah I know!"

"Is it me?" Here we go again.

"Whadda you think?"

"I don't know. That's why I'm askin'. I mean, you shouldn't even be worryin' about me, with all of those other women swarmin' around you."

"Soma…honey…babygirl, I already toldja, those are just clients that I give dance lessons to."

"Is?!" she snorted. Then, "It don't matter. It don't even matter. We just need to give each other some space." By this time in the conversation, I was beginning to have a panic attack. Couldn't imagine her breaking up with me. I had to put an end to this situation real quick.

Quietly, I asked, "So…is it somebody else?" Silence on her end.

"Hello?"
"No." Yeah, right.
"Girl, you ain't gotta lie. This is Al you're talkin' to. Tell me the truth."
"No, it ain't nobody else."
"You sure?"
"I told you…no! Well…"
"What?"

She took a deep breath and paused. The silence seemed like an eternity. Then, "Yeah, there is," she finally admitted.

My heart dropped, but my voice rose to a roar. "Goddammit, why'd you lie then?" My heart was pounding by now, and my stomach was churning like a homemade ice cream maker. But I couldn't control myself, and I had to start up.

"Why couldn't you just come out and tell me?"
"You didn't tell me about Turion," she snapped. "I knew that once you got to college, it'd be someone else. I had to look out for me. Knew you wouldn't understand."

"What the hell is there to understand?" I roared. "You're leavin' me because of what happened at the show?"

"No!" she shot back. "I'm leaving you because I can't not be thinking about how you might be screwing someone else. I can't trust you anymore."

You know what? The more black men get excited, the higher our voice becomes. By now, I sounded like Chris Tucker, all high and whiny like a mosquito.

"Oh, this some bullshit! How you gonna lie and say that we need space, and then finally admit that it's because of the fact that you're seein' somebody else? And then, gonna try and blame it on the talent show, and 'cuz I'm givin' dance lessons that I'm screwin' other women? Man, that shit is so unfair! So who is ol' boy?"

"You don't know him."
"I bet I do. He go to any one of the schools in the A.U.C.?"
"Maybe." Goddammit, Soma!
"Why are you bein' so vague? Why can't you tell me anything about him? How long you been seein' him? Can I ask that? Will you tell me that?"

"Mmmm...maybe about two months." By now she was so calm and so nonchalant. I just wanted to reach through the phone and strangle her. Calm down Al.

"I see. Well, are you fuckin' this man or what?" I asked.

"Mmm...don't think that should be a concern of yours. You know, since you've got other women." I got mad then.

"Goddamn," I exhaled. "You ARE fuckin' this man, ain'tcha? Why?" Again, here she went with the nonchalantness.

"Okay, so why you so concerned now? You wasn't thinkin' about me then when you were givin' your so-called 'dance lessons' to your other women, now were ya?"

"What the fuck are you talkin' about, Soma? For the last time, I'm NOT FUCKIN' ANYBODY BUT YOU!! And as to the reason as to why I'm so concerned, I'll tell ya…'cuz I'm your MAN, Soma!! Your muthafuckin' man!" Then she tried to play the victim.

"Were," she said. "Were. Who you were and what we were doing is now past tense." She sighed. "Al, I …I can't talk about this right now. You are really stressin' me out."

Ain't that a bitch? "You know what?" I started in, "You got a lot of nerve. *You're* stressed out right now?! You?! My woman's fuckin' with somebody else over some paranoid bullshit that you have absolutely no proof of, and she's stressed. Fuck you, Soma! If you really cared about my ass, then you woulda asked questions instead of jumpin' the fuckin' gun!"

Then in the middle of this storm, her father decided to pick up the phone. Apparently he heard all the yelling going on by me, and decided that this was the time he was gonna step in and save the day. Super Dad, huh? Get the fuck outta here.

"Okay, you two…what's going on?" Soma's bravado fell like trees cut down in the Amazon.

"Oh, um, n-n-nothin' Daddy."

"Al?"

"Nothing sir."

"Well, I heard all of this hoopin' and hollerin' from my daughter," he continued. "And then I hear all of this screaming that you doin'. So again I ask…what's goin' on? Soma?"

"Daddy, it's nothin'."

"Like she said sir, nothin'."

"Well it'd better be nothin'. That or get your ass kicked if you hurt my daughter." Kick whose ass? That old man? Please!

"Whatever," I said, under my breath. But the old man could hear very well.

"You said somethin', young blood?" he questioned.

"No sir, not me."

"Thought so," he said, trash talkin'. I heard him hang up the phone. Finally. Now back to us. I still couldn't get over this shit.

"Soma," I started again at room level, "I can't believe that you are doin' this to me."

"Well, you should've thought about that when you decided to start screwing those other girls." Here she went again. I had to stop and correct her for her benefit.

"For the last damn time, I wasn't screwin'…"

"What about Torion?"

"What? What about her? She's just a friend. Let me place emphasis on it again… a FRIEND. That's all."

"Just a friend, huh?"

"Yeah! It's just like I keep tellin' you, but you don't wanna listen. I aim not seein', creepin' with, or freakin' anybody else. I'm in love with you! YOU! Can't you see that?"

Silence on both our part. Then "You still don't believe me, huh?"

"Al," she began. "When this separation is over, maybe we can try again. You know, get back to normal. Until then…"

My stomach was really starting to act up now. She was really leaving me.

"Don't do this to me, girl," I begged.

"Do what? I ain't done nothin' to you, and maybe that's the problem. But like I said, until we get this worked out…I…I don't wanna see you." My stomach stopped hurting, and I started getting angry.

"So that's your final say-so?" I asked.

"That's what I'm saying." I was furious on the inside, but I remained calm. I couldn't do nothin' about it, which frustrated me even more.

"All right then. I guess I'll just see you around sometimes…maybe."

"Maybe. Good-bye, Al." She hung up the phone, and didn't even give me a chance to say good-bye. She was gone, just like that, and I was convicted of a crime.

No jury, no trial. Just sentencing over a crime that I didn't commit.

I was hurt bad. I couldn't sleep. I wouldn't sleep. I cried and I didn't sleep for seven straight days. This was one of the first of many times that I would experience this type of heartbreak. But it was the *first* time. I was fuckin' up in school. I started drinking, and couldn't remember our routines at our dance group's rehearsal and just leave. At one point, I even called her mom and begged for her to help me make it through this dilemma. But her mom was a trip, too. You know what this arrogant bat said? Check this out:

"I'm sorry, Al, but I really don't think I can help you with this." Ain't that some shit? I was like, "But you're her mom! You're like one of the closest people to her on the planet. Plus she listens to you. So maybe you could step in to help with this situation."

"Well, I may be her mother, but I make it a point to not interfere in my daughter's affairs. Now, as far as you two go, she had a right to make that decision of breaking up, but that's on her." Facts, but at the same time, in my young mind, I really thought that she would have gave in and helped, but she didn't. So raw and so uncaring.

I was like, "So there ain't nothin' you can do? Come on now, I'm sure that at least one point in your life you fell deeply in love with a man. How'd you handle it?"

"I married him."

"Ohhh, okay. But Mrs. Trite, hear me out. I ain't slept in seven days. I mean, this thing is really tearin' me up right about now. What would you do? Would you please reconsider and help me? Please?"

She hesitated. Then, "Okay, Al. For your sake, I'll see what I can do." I perked up a little bit. It's what I needed to hear.

"Really? You promise?" I was psyched.

"Like I said, I'll see what I can do," answered Ms. Haughty slash Arrogant Mother Number One. "But I ain't makin' no promises." But I didn't care about her attitude. All I knew was that she agreed to help me.

"Mrs. Trite, thank you. Thank you so freakin' much. Can we keep this a secret between us, though? I don't want Soma to know that I asked for your help." I could actually hear her rolling her eyes as I said that.

"Honey, my lips are sealed."

" Great. Thank you again, Mrs. Trite. Appreciate you so much."

"Okay. Good bye now, Al."

"Good bye." I hung up the phone. Triflin' arrogant ass momma.

So I waited. One day went by. No call. Two days, then three. A full week came and went. Still no call. I was on pins and needles again and the stomach definitely started churnin' like butter again. Finally, the Wednesday into the second week, the phone rang. I jumped to that sucker and damn near broke my ankle in the process. I took a deep breath and then answered.

"Hello?"

"Hello, Al?"

"Yes?"

"Guess who?"

"Don't have to. Whassup?"

"Nothin' much." Pause. "I, uh…started not to call you."

"Yeah? Well what changed your mind?"

"Don't know. I was mad at you, though."

"Mad at me? Why?"

"You know why. 'Cuz it was real messed up that you went behind my back and asked my mom to talk to me about us. To 'smooth things out', as you would say." At that point I really hated her momma. She was like a bucket with a damn hole in it. Dammit! I played it cool, though.

"What'chu talkin' 'bout, girl? I didn't…"

"Hey. Hey! Lemme tell you somethin' real quick," she said, cutting me off. "Nobody decides what's best for me, but me. You got that?"

"But I didn't…"

"You got that?!"

"Yeah, Soma. I got it." Damn Hellcat. Thought that agreeing would shut her up. It didn't.

"I mean, who the hell do you think you are, bringin' my mother into my personal affairs?" she continued. "That definitely won't bring us back together. It just pushes me away even farther to the point of not even wanting to get back with you again. I like to keep my business private, and if I wanted my mom's help, I woulda asked for it."

"I understand that, Soma," I said, trying to save face, "But I love you."

"Well you can love me all day long, but right now, love ain't got nothin' to do with this. If you really loved and understood me, then you would've just waited for me to give you a call instead of tryin' to get help to try and fix the situation."

"And how long would that have taken?"

"Oh, it wouldn't have taken long at first. I started reconsidering, but now, you and I are the last thing to worry about." Damn, why does she keep trying me?

"Well, shit," I countered. "You think I've got all year to wait?"

" Oh naw, absolutely not. Matter of fact, here's some advice for you, Al. You might wanna move on, 'cuz after this, I'm definitely getting ready to. I'm done with this."

Damn.

Soma had officially dropped the Big One, the one that wiped out everything. My head felt light, and my heart started pounding. I was on the verge of crying, but I didn't. We held the phone for a long, long time. The only sound was breathing on both ends. Finally, I found the words to speak.

"So, just like that? You're just gonna drop everything that we've meant to each other all this time?"

Young, Black, Talented, & Alone
49

"Believe me, the decision wasn't easy. But when you called my mom, that was the icing on the cake. That last straw that broke the camel's back." I got mad.

"Ay, you ain't gotta quote those sayings to me, 'cuz I know 'em all. Yeah, I'm sure it really wasn't easy coming to that decision with that other man to occupy your time and lay up with. I'm pretty sure the only reason you did call was 'cuz your mom pissed you off, because yes, I did come to her for help. But so what? If your momma hadn't talked to you, I know for a fact that I probably wouldn't haven't been another thought in that pretty little pinhead of yours now, would I?" I shot back.

"And that's why I'm not with you now," she snapped. Okay, that hurt. I couldn't let her get away with that shit.

"Excuse me? And what exactly is 'why'?" I questioned.

"Because you told my business. Because you won't give us space to breathe."

"Okay, now what the fuck are *you* talkin' about? I must've missed something. Let's not forget that *you're* the one that jumped up for air and then came back down holding your breath with another dude. Just exactly what do you see in this man?" Oh yeah, it was getting' ugly. But Soma could be ugly, too.

"Well, the best thing about him is that he's nothin' like you."

"I know," I replied sarcastically. "Because if he was, then you'd still be with me, now wouldn't ya?"

She ignored me. "He's kind, caring, has his own transportation, and best of all...he's older."

"Oh, okay. I see now."

"What? What you see, Al?"

"I see it. The whole big picture. Because he got a car and is older...that's why you're with him. That's also the reason why you're probably fucking him, too."

"Nope. That's not true."

"Yes it is, but it's all right. I can get a job, too. And as far as the bus is concerned? The bus may not be as good as your own ride, but I'll tell you what: Before you met ol' boy, you didn't have a problem goin' from one place to another with me on MARTA, now didja? Long as I paid your fare, you didn't say shit. You just rode." That shut her up real quick right then. It was so quiet, I thought that she had put the phone down to do something else.

"Hello?" I called out.

"Yeah, Al, you can believe whatever you want, but I need a man, not a boy. Someone who can..."

"So now I'm just a boy?"

She continued. "Someone who can handle business on all ends, not just in the bed." Now *that* shit hurt. I thought that I was good to her, that we were good together, but obviously she didn't.

"Soma," I said quietly. "You go to hell for that remark. I ain't got a car, but that don't mean I'm beneath you, either."

"Did I say that?" she shot back. "All I said is that I needed a man who…"

"I heard what the fuck you said!" I stated.

"Watch your mouth."

"Yeah, okay. Sorry. I think you've said enough." We both got quiet then.

"So," she started, "What you wanna do?"

"What I wanna do? Have you been listening to me? Can you read between the lines?"

"No."

"Damn! At least you're honest. Soma, in spite of all of this I wanna be with you again. Can't you see that? Obviously not, 'cuz you see what you wanna see."

"Not true."

"Is true, 'cuz you ain't feelin' me right now. That should have been the first thing that should have been obvious. I've been tryin' to get you back!"

"I hear ya, but I still need breathing room."

"No you don't. You still wanna experiment while you have time, before you settle down. You hear this?" I rattled a sheet of paper. "This is a marriage contract, and I was hoping that we'd be together long enough for you to sign it. But now," I said, tearing up the paper, "I guess not."

"Al…" Long pause. "Al, are you still there? Don't do this." It almost sounded like she was having a change of heart.

"Why shouldn't I? It's obvious that your love for me ain't there no more, and I can't see you wanting to be with me, but it's cool. That's always how it is before brothas establish themselves and become successful. Then that same woman that rejected the brotha the first time tries to make a comeback. But in the case of us," I continued, "Ain't gonna be no comeback. Remember Soma, you chose to do this. But remember, we all pay for what we do in the end."

"Al…"
"Soma," I paused, "I have to go now. Take care."
"But see, Al, you…"

I just hung up the phone and exhaled. I was more angry at the fact that I let myself get to this point of letting my true feelings out, and then letting myself get out of pocket with the situation, and let her pull me in there. From that point on, I vowed that I would never ever call Soma again. EVER.

Another Round,
Shawty

Two months went by, and eventually time began to heal my wounds. It felt strange. Here I was at first trying to reconcile, to make everything alright, and now I didn't even feel myself longing for her. I didn't give a damn what she was doing, I didn't care who she was seeing, and most of all, if she never called again, then good riddance.

You know, it really hurts a man's ego not when his woman leaves him, but when he can picture in his mind somebody else getting water from his fountain. That right there is enough to make any brotha go crazy, and I must admit, it did screw with my head for a minute. But only for a minute though. Guess that's why there are a lot of crimes of passion. I watch Snapped. Even though I said good riddance, I still couldn't picture nobody else with my girl. That was really fucked up, 'cuz I let her go. But I damn sure didn't pick up that phone to call, believe that.

At the beginning of the third month, she finally called in.

"Hey." Hey? Hey is for horses.

"Hey. Who is this?" She got pissed then.

"Who's this? Who's this?" she spouted.

"That's what I said." I was being a smart-ass, but I didn't care. "Who…is…this?"

"Really? I know we haven't spoken for a minute, Al, but this is Soma."

"Oh…hey Soma. How you doin'?"

"I'm good. Don't you recognize my voice anymore?"

Dryly, I was like, "No, not really. You kinda sounded like...nevermind. So what's up?"

"Whaat? Nothin'. I was just thinkin' about you, so I decided to give you a call."

"Really? Well, to be honest with you, I haven't really thought about us since I signed off." She paused. From that point, I knew that she was trippin', based on the previous drama. She picked up the conversation again.

"Okay, I'll take that. But I had to call you, because I had to let you know that what you said came true."

"Oh? And what was that?"

"Well, it's like you said...you truly do reap what you sow. I just wanted to let you know that I'm sorry. For everything. I'm sorry for all that I did and said to you, and I really do miss you. I want you back in my life so bad, so I'm putting my pride to the side, and asking you if you would reconsider coming back." Soma must've lost her damn mind. Not so fast, though.

"Why?" I stated. "Why should I, when you put me through all of this mess in the first place?"

"Because I finally came to the realization of who I loved." Shit.

"Love?" I snorted. This was my opportunity to unleash the beast and tear into that ass about how I felt. "The fuck you know about love? The kind of unconditional love you had from me in the beginning, but were so stupid being paranoid that you threw it all away when you had it? Is that the kind of love that you're talking about?"

"Yes." I know that she felt small, 'cuz I broke her ass down to the ground.

"Well tell me this: What do you really know about love?"

"I don't know. I just know that I love you. That's all."

"Really? Well, I remember at one point you told me that you moved on."

"And your point is?"

"My point is this: What was it that changed your mind? That brotha that you were so into had a car, a job, money...everything you could ask for. So what was it that made you leave his ass? He probably wasn't fuckin' you right, huh?"

"That's not the point, and whatever happened happened. I simply realized who my heart belonged to."
"Is that right?"
"Yeah. It is."

"I see. Hmmm." I laid down on my bed. "So what'cha wanna do about this?" Heavy sigh on her end. Then, "I wanna be with you. Total commitment and everything. You're just gonna have to trust me."

I was outdone. "What? Trust you?" I retorted. "Why? Who the hell you think you talkin' to? I was born at night, but not last night. Why should I trust you now?" I could feel the wounds opening up again, and I was beginning to feel the pain. That conversation was like hot knives stabbing me in my chest.

"Because," she started. "Because…I can't tell you. I can't tell you, and I can't describe why you should. All I know is that when I was with that other person, it just didn't feel right."

"And that's how you know that you wanted to be with me again? Because it didn't feel right?" I could hear her exhale. Good. I wanted her to feel how I felt.

"Al, I know that I put you through hell, and I deserve it if you never, ever talk to me again, but if you come back, I mean it when I say that I can change."

"Oh really? How can I be sure? How do I know that you're just not talkin' outta the side of your neck to get me back?" I questioned.

"Once again, you're just gonna have to trust me." Long-ass pause on my part.

"Well, listen," she said. "I'm not tryin' to put you on the spot anymore than you already are, so I'll tell you what. I'll give you a week to decide what you wanna do. If you don't call me back, then I'll just take it that you moved on, and I'll just leave well enough alone. Is that fair?"

"Yeah that's fair."

"Good. So I'll talk to you later, 'kay?"

"Yeah, okay. Whatever." I hung up the phone and then the reality of the situation hit me. Soma was really wanting to get back with a brotha, even after all of this bullshit. After her ass lied and gave me the wrong reasons for leaving. After giving me freakin' migraines, keeping my stomach churning, and keeping me up for seven straight days with no sleep, just worryin' about us. After she lied and said that she wasn't kickin' it or sleepin with nobody, and she was. And now wanting to get back with me with full and complete devotion, after a light came on to show her that she really loved me? I just couldn't figure that shit out. I thought about her offer all week long, talked to friends who were *so* damn blunt about it. They were like, "Sheeet, you ain't got nothin' to lose. Better hit it and quit it, and then be out." Talked to my sister, and finally prayed over it.

You know, in the Bible, a Christian is supposed to forgive, and turn the other cheek. Well, I could forgive superficially, but I damn sure couldn't forget. All I thought about was how in the past me and Soma used to be. Used to be. That was key, because that was past, and somewhere in my heart, I just felt that you couldn't go back to the past, because things never revert back to being the same. I also felt that once a leopard, always a leopard, because it never ever changes its spots. In short, I had a gut feeling that Soma was just gonna break away from me again and leave me back where I started…in heartbreak and heartache. I didn't know. I just didn't know. But being a man, I listened to my head, and…I…took…her…BACK.

I must admit, for the first month, I was suspicious and paranoid, just like she was. She flooded me with attention, though. She would always call and tell me where she was going or what she was doing in order to avoid my suspicion and also for me to build my trust. Mind you, she did not have to report to me. That was her decision. It eventually got on my nerves. I guess I became bitter, too, because every time I was with her (in the Biblical sense), all I could think about was her and that brotha screwin', and a lot of times it would get to me, 'cuz I was always throwin' it up in her face. Shit, even in bed, I kept throwin' it up. She could be on top, just moanin', and I'd get mad. After she got hers, and it was my turn to be on top, I'd just be talkin' trash.

"Did he do it like this? Was it good like this? Whose is it? WHOSE IS IT? Did you call out that brotha's name like you do mine? Huh? Answer me, goddamn it! Who's your daddy? WHO'S YOUR MU'FUCKIN' DADDY?!" To my surprise, with all my negativity, her answers were positive. I guess that she was doing everything she could to get back in good with me, and I guess over time again, it worked. I eventually stopped comparing myself to that brotha and stopped throwin' up all that resentment, and finally settled in. After all, she wasn't with that brotha no more, so it didn't matter.

Or did it?

Somehow, somewhere, I had this gut feeling that Soma was gonna eventually slip. And you know what? The gut was right. Shit, the gut is always right.

Emotions + Likka= Gas on a Fire

We had been goin' good again for the past eight months. I was looking at the prospect of marriage again with her. We were both talkin' about it, and started spending more and more time with each other. She was really, really trying to make it work, I could tell. However, I knew that it was just a matter of time before she strayed. Knew it. After all, she was young, fine, and naïve, but still dinghy. Somebody gives her a compliment, and she's on Cloud Nine, and then the next thing you know, she's buck-assed naked after a couple more. Sadly, I turned out to be right.

That ninth month was officially the beginning of the end for me and Soma. Officially. Remember when I mentioned that when Soma was trying to get back in like Flynn, she would always call me and let me know where she was and what she was doing? I had gotten so used to her calling that it became habitual for me to hear from her daily before she did anything. In that ninth month, it slowly started to slack off. Also, the amount of calls and conversation began to fall off. And then the time spent…where the hell did that go?

She had changed again. Sometimes I wonder if Soma had multiple personalities like white folk, 'cuz she damn sure acted like she did. She went from always wanting to spend time (and planning events to do) to almost dwindling down to next to none. Now, I would really rarely hear from her, and when she did call, the conversation would be dull, boring, and listless on her side. She'd grow impatient and would just be like, "Anything else?," and I'd be like, "No," and that would be it. After a couple more months, we were just tryin' to hang on, screwing to keep things alive, but the gut feeling I had never left. Our calls became or started becoming slim to none, and I guess we both realized that maybe letting things be as they should've been when we were separated would've been the best thing to do.

But I just couldn't let the booty go…

I started to ask myself exactly where did we go wrong? As I searched through the mental files, I couldn't discover it. I mean, everybody goes through problems in a relationship, some big, some small. Believe me, we both had our share. I was a little bit more temperamental, but that was because I was in love for the first time in my life and I just wanted her to do right. Plus, I was serious, and looking back, I didn't think she really was. I think that the prospect of wanting to get married to her was too much for her to handle. I know it was. Most sisters at that age generally aren't ready for a commitment like that. They just wanna keep fishing until they get the biggest bass, not the tiniest minnow, and I could tell that Soma had put her pole in the water again. I guess she just had it in her mind that I just couldn't let things go about her relationship with Otha Brotha, so without really talking to me about where we stood, she went out and started dating Otha Brotha again. I found this out through some of my other friends that knew us. They had starting seeing her everywhere with him, and reported back to me. In spite of that, she was still letting me come over there late night, sneaking through the back of the house at the sliding glass door and letting me hit it. At that point, our relationship was becoming purely physical.

As long as I was taggin' that ass, it didn't matter who she dated, 'cuz she assured me that I was the only one who she was giving it to. She even lied to my face that she wasn't dating anybody else *while* I was hittin' it. Like I believed that shit. My friends knew that I was still in love with her, and they also knew that she was making a fool out of me (this was before she became just a late-night booty call). They knew I wouldn't believe what they said because she and I had been through so much, and what she promised, so they did what they had to do. They got me drunk one night ('cuz they knew when I got drunk I clowned). I mean, really, pissy, tore-up-from-the-floor-up drunk. Then they decided that we were gonna just roll out and take me. While my intentions were that we were gonna just go to a party on Morehouse's campus, their ideas were very different. They wanted me to see with my own eyes just how much of a player Soma was, and since I wasn't in my right mind and listening to my inner self, I was gung ho on going and REALLY seein' what it was all about. In looking back, that had to be one of the worse nights of my life since I've existed.

We're now in the car, and they just kept talkin' trash. They were tellin' me that Soma was no good, that she was just a ho who couldn't care less about me, that the only reason she was with me was because I was a reliable safety net of balancing her out, the only fool who would go back every time and give her what she wanted; all she had to do was ask. They talked trash about seeing her with a lot of older men, men that looked like they were old enough to be her daddy, including Ol' Boy.

Dirty old men with money…

I must admit, I damn sure didn't believe them, but the alcohol won me over. Can you believe that as drunk as I was, I was the one drivin? They made me so mad, and got me so fired up that I was getting ready to put these Negroes outta my car. How you gonna talk trash to the driver and ride? Shit!

I pulled over with the quickness to put 'em out, and they quickly became apologetic. Apologetic, yes, but still puttin' those thoughts in my head. They were like, "Hey, we're sorry about what we said, but you don't think she's messin' around?"

"Nah, I don't think so. Hell, she better not be! We just got back together!"

"We feel ya," said Terrence, "But we ain't stupid. We got love for ya, and that's why we're tellin' you this. Some of us have actually seen Soma with other brothas."

"When?" I questioned.

"Just in the last week!"

"Nah," I said. "Can't be. Can't be true."

"You don't think so?" Terrence continued. "Okay. Let's go over there right now, then."

Anger and hurt welled up inside of me. I wanted to prove

Terrence wrong. Hell, I wanted to prove all of them wrong. We just got reunited, and it felt so good. I didn't want to believe any more than what Terrence and the rest of the crew were saying, so I did the next best thing.

"A'ight. Let's roll."

We were doin' eighty miles an hour all the way
to her house in a residential neighborhood, where the
speed limit was 35. I rushed over there, because Soma
told me earlier that tonight she was just going to be
chillin', not doing anything or going anywhere. I was as
wrong as white Mormons moving into the projects to
talk about Jesus. We got there at about ten-thirty, and
damn if these fool weren't right!

Ol' Boy's car was sittin' in the driveway, and
Soma was sitting in there with him. The emotions began
to roll, only this time, they were magnified over a
thousand times, and they came out very
slllloooowwwwwllyyy. Aannngerrr. Jealllloussssssyy.
Paaannniiic. God bless those spirits that give liquid
courage!

The boys couldn't wait to start throwing it in my
face about how right they were. All of them were like,
"See? We told you! Didn't we tell you?" I knew they
were right , but I didn't know what I was going to do. I
pulled up right next to dude's car in the driveway and
opened up the door. I called myself getting out, but I
literally fuckin' fell flat on my face on the concrete.
Then the car started to roll. In trying to see what I was
gonna do, Mikey had his knee on the emergency brake,
and had pressed it down. Brothas started screamin'.
Soma's eyes got wide, and I tried to help myself from
the ground up. Thank God one of the other brothas had
sense enough to grab and pull up the parking brake in
my shit. Seeing that the car was stopped, I stumbled over
to Ol' Boy's car, around to the passenger side where
Soma was sitting.

"Soma!" I yelled out. I could hear her say,
"Ohhh shit."

Otha Brotha got defensive, like he was gonna fight or somethin'. I wish he would've. My crew would've beat his ass. He was like, "Who is that?" to Soma as I stumbled and tried to hold myself on Soma's door.

"Nobody. He's nobody," as I stood there.

"Nobody? Bitch, who the fuck you think you talkin' to?" I asked. "I'll show you 'nobody'!" She turned to Otha Brotha.

"Does this window roll up automatically?" she asked him.

"Yeah."

"Well, can you start rolling it up, please? Just roll it up and don't say…"

Boy, for a drunk, I was quick. As soon as it started rolling up, I grabbed that sucka and forced it down. Dammit, that night, Soma was *gonna* talk to me.

"Soma," I began slowly, "Why the fuck are you trippin'? Why you lie and say you wasn't going nowhere, but you're out here in the driveway with this brotha? What's up with that?"

"Al, I don't owe you any explanation. I'll talk to you later."

"No hell you won't , 'cuz there ain't gonna be a 'later'." Then Otha Brotha decided that he was gonna butt into my conversation.

"Look, man…" he began.

"Ay, shut the fuck up. Ain't nobody talkin' to your ass. This is between me and Soma."

"What you say, mu'fucka?! I'll beat your ass!" he exclaimed, starting to get out of his car. Yeah, come on.

"Come with it then, brotha, but look around you. You gon' have to beat my ass, and then my boys. Look over there." I pointed to my car. He looked, and by that time, the fellas had gotten out of the car and were standing in the driveway with their arms crossed, ready for action.

"Sure you wanna take that ride?" I asked. Soma was disgusted.

Guess what? He saved himself from a bona-fide ass-whuppin' that night.

"Soma," he asked, "Who is this?"

"Who is this?" I said. "I should be asking you that question! I'm her boyfriend, punk, who are you?"

"Ex-boyfriend!" she said. "We were just trying to get things together, but now, Al, I want you to know that we are not together anymore."

I was truly fuckin' hurt. "Oh, so what? I'm just your fuckboy, whenever you need a piece?" Ol' Boy's eyes widened.

"So *you're* Al!" he asked in amazement. He looked at Soma, and Soma looked back.

"This the crazy mu'fucka you were talkin' about?"

"Crazy?!" I glared at Soma. She couldn't even look at me. Who else knows what she had told him? That shit pissed me off.

"So I'm crazy, huh? I'll show you crazy!"
She started trying to roll up the window again, but I grabbed it and forced it down. Then she started yelling to Otha Brotha, "Drive, just drive!" This fool shifted into reverse, and then, not being in my right mind, I jumped on the hood.

"Bitch, you...ain't...goin'...nowhere!" I screamed. I remember Soma looking at me wide-eyed through the windshield, tugging on Ol' Boy's arm to make him go faster. Still, I didn't let go.

He peeled down the driveway, and I hit the pavement hard, rolling down the hill. Someone had crunk up my car and rolled down the hill to get me. The next few events are foggy. I remember someone looking up at me, then the rest of my crew clamoring around me.
"Damn, you all right?"

"Let's get him in the car," someone else said. By this time, I didn't want anybody to touch me.
"Get offa me!" I yelled. But they grabbed me, threw me in the car, got in and got the hell on. Maurieus was driving. Mikey started fussing me out.

"You stupid mu'fucka! Why you go and make an ass outta yourself?" he said. "'Cuz if that was me, I woulda said, 'fuck you bitch!' a long time ago!"

All this shit while I'm layin' on the back seat, bleedin' from falling off the car. Slowly I formed the words, "Don't nobody understand. I love her." Maurieus almost ran the car into a ditch when he heard me say that. He pulled over, and looked at me.

"What? You still love that bitch, even after that bullshit just went down? I *know* you're just talkin' shit. Either that, or your ass is obsessed!"

"Whatever. Drive back there and see if she came back."
"Are you serious, man?"
"Just do it!"

Maurieus whipped the car back around, and we rolled back to her house and pulled in the lower end of the driveway. All of us got out.
"I can't believe she did this to me," I said, looking around.

"Believe it. That's how life is sometimes."
"Man, I really thought she loved me."
"Horse shit! That bitch too stupid to know what love is."
"Yeah, I guess. But it's still fucked up."
"Life is fucked up."

A light came on from Soma's house. We heard Raging Richard yell out, "What's going on out here?" That's when one of the dumb-asses I was with decided to holler back.

"Get'cho ass back in the house, old man!"

"What?" came the reply.

"You heard me!" Dumb-Ass Number One shot back. The light went out. Then silence. We started laughing.

"That ol' man betta keep his ass in the house," said Mikey.

Then came the unmistakable sound of a shotgun being pumped. Boy, I ain't never been dragged so fast, nor can I remember when the Dumb-Ass Crew or my car moved so fast. Them brothas literally threw my ass in the car and rolled the fuck out. I passed out, but not for long. Brothas were like, "Damn, man." "Sorry for ya, man." "Fool, you need to cheer up...and quick!" One of 'em said, "I know, right? Hey, let's roll on over to Morehouse. They're havin' a party." I don't remember if I said, "Cool" or what, but the next thing I know, we're there. And yes, it was live. Honeys everywhere. The guys stepped out and started walking. I stepped out, started walking...and then fell down the outside steps leading to the party. People coming in and going out were passing me by, asking my crew, "Is he all right?," and I was like, "What...'chall...lookin'...at?" Talkin' shit and still layin' on the ground.

"He's fine, don't worry about it," said Marieus, picking me up with the quickness. "Come on." The next thing I know, we're sitting in the car, and I'm drunker than a monkey in one of those spinning G-force contraptions at NASA.

"Marieus…" I heard myself say.

"What?"

"Marieus…"

"What, man?" He was getting annoyed.

"Man…I'm hungrier than a mu'fucka. I gotta get me somethin' to eat." I held out my hand. "Gimme my keys."

He looked at me like I had just escaped from the looney bin. "What? You must be outta yo damn mind. You are in no condition to drive." He held up the keys. "I'll hold on to these, and *I'll* drive."

"Oh yeah? Well then, ha!" I snatched them out of his hand. "You think that it's gonna be just that damn easy just for you to come in and take my damn…" He punched me in the stomack, and then took them right back.

"Ouch! Shit!" I moved over to the other side of the car. "Hey man, that shit hurt!"

He paid me no mind, just started up the car.

"A'ight, let's go." And then just like that, we were out.

We rolled up to Wendy's, where I ordered a triple value meal, a large order of straws, and a "big-ass order of napkins." While we were waiting , I started to ramble. You know, drunk talk. The kind of talk where anything you think makes sense comes up and ultimately out. Where you go from one thought to the next, but *verrry slowwwly.*

"Yo, Mari," I started up.

"What?"

"Man. I love you, man."

"Stop trippin', brotha."

"Naw, I ain't trippin'. I really…love you, man."

"Yo Al man, shut yo' ass up. Stop that shit right now. You hear me?"

"Stop what? Man…I ain't…" The next thing I know, it's morning, and I'm laying in my bed, clothes still on me. I've got the biggest hangover in history, and I've got cottonmouth like hell. The only thing I didn't do was pray to the porcelain god, and I couldn't. However, that wild night still didn't do diddley for trying to erase the pain I had of seein' the woman I was in love with be with another man, no matter how many drinks I had. Bein' with him (screwing him, having him take her out to eat, screwing him…screwing him), that's all I could think about. The whole experience was just too painful at my expense, and all these thoughts came at once. After I looked out the window, and saw that my dad's car was parked in the driveway safely and in one piece, I made the resolution this morning that once and for all I would just stop dealin' with Soma the best way I knew how…and that was to just go cold turkey on her ass. I knew it wouldn't be easy, but it had to be done in order to keep me from just goin' fuckin' crazy.

Doing that, I started getting depressed again. Whenever I couldn't find anything to do was when my mind started to wander. That's when I would think about the times that we had together. Damn, I was at such a crucial slope in my life!! I put away her individual

Young, Black, Talented, & Alone
73

pictures, put away the pictures that we had taken together, tried to bury it all in my closet, but every time I turned around, there was always *something* that reminded me of her. Anything from songs on the radio to what I ate for dinner, to the type of clothing I wore, to cars on the street, to even bus stops...*all* of that shit reminded me of Soma. I even started *dreamin'* of me and her together again, makin' love in my room, and in the morning on more than one occasion, I'd have to wash my sheets.

This shit went on for a month and a half, before the spell she cast on me wore off. Oh yeah, and during that time, she didn't call. This junk went on for the whole summer, and down here in the South, when it gets hot, brothas get horny. And I was horny as hell. And her ass *still didn't call.* But I guess that we both needed this experience, simply because we needed to get on with our lives. She was trying to move on, and I needed to break free. But before we closed the book on us, there was one more event that needed to be included. And that event was the one that sealed the deal and got us both fucked up.

Exodus

Remember when I stated earlier that me and Soma were like soul mates, and that we could almost predict each other's actions and words without failure? Probably not, but we could. Seriously. I could tell what was on her mind before she even said it. The same could be said of her, and that was a good thing, even if only for a minute. Then came the agony of her cheatin' on me, destroying all of my hopes and dreams, and just basically becoming my first real-life lesson in this cold, cruel world of what we call relationships. Anyway, with all of that said and done, I had to bring closure. We had to bring closure to our situation, because this business of her seein' Otha Brotha, and using me for a sex object was beginning to get old real quick. I mean, I knew the situation I was in, and yes I know that I put myself out there…but I was still in love with her ass, and that made me a fool. Soma could've said, "Jump!," and I would've said, "On what style? Kriss Kross or House of Pain? Awwww, Soma make me wanna…jump jump!" Am I stupid? Yeah! "Jump, jump!"

So I had to bring closure to this shit. Don't get me wrong, I liked the thrill of sneaking in her house and mixing it up with her on the living room floor while her parents were upstairs knocked out. I liked the fact of her comin' to the sliding-glass door with nothing on but a robe and being butt-naked underneath, primed and ready for action. Hell, I liked the fact of not havin' to wear any drawers when I came over there, just unzip, strip, and be ready for some freaky-deeky in a heartbeat. I enjoyed her moaning, my moaning, us tonguing, just me and her stripped down to the bone, and getting primal.

Doin' it all types of ways. Cowgirl. Doggystyle. Missionary. Sideways. T.V. watchin' style (ya'll ain't never heard of that one before, but you know as black people, we tend to get highly creative, so whazzup?) Oral. The way she made me feel. And the way she made me cum so unbelievably hard. Dammit, I loved it all, but it HAD TO STOP. My feelings for her were definitely starting to come back. Hell, they WERE back, 'cuz I was starting to fall in love all over again.

Actually, I could honestly say that my feelings never actually went away, and neither did the fire. I remember when we were broken up on one of her birthdays, how we said that we were going to just try and be friends, and I ended up taking her to see Prince in concert on his LoveSexy tour. She loved it…and that night that friend junk went straight out the window. The next day after that, we were right back at it, her fussing about not wanting a commitment, me arguing about trying to stay together. Didn't matter, though, because we were still ending up in bed.

That's what I was thinking about the next-to-last time that we were getting busy. Usually, I'm talkin' dirty to her, but tonight I was just quiet while she did her.
"What's wrong?," she asked. Great, she finally noticed I wasn't speaking.
"Nothin'."
"Then why aren't you talkin' to me or slappin' my ass or something?"
"It's nothin'. I'm just tired, that's all."
"You sure?"
"Positive."

"'Kay." She went back to ridin' out again, right on humpin' with nothing else to say. When she finally came and laid down next to me, I couldn't take it. I got up, put on my pants and left, without ever saying a word. Didn't even kiss her like I usually did, even though she puckered up for it. When she heard the sliding-glass door open up, she opened up her eyes and looked at me in disbelief as I snuck back out. I swear, as soon as I got home, the phone rang. Two-thirty in the morning, and I lived with Mom and Pop.

"Hello?" I said.

"Hello?" my mom answered.

"Ma, it's just Soma callin' to see if I made it in."

"Hi, Mrs. Alexander. It's me, Soma."

"Hey Soma," my mom responded. "I thought that Al wasn't dating you any…"

"Okayyyy. Goodnight, Ma," I said, trying to cut her off.

"Listen, Al, don't you tell me no 'goodnight'. This is MY phone. I pay this bill. So if anybody should be sayin' goodnight, it should be *you*." With that, she hung it up. Soma started in on me.

"So, what was wrong with you tonight?"

"I told you nothing," I spat at her. "Didn't I tell you that before I left?"

"Actually, you didn't say nothin' to me at all," she shot back. "So, I felt the need to call, because you aren't normally the quiet type."

"Oh yeah?" I said. "Well, y'know Soma, sometimes it's best to be quiet. Sometimes silence is golden." She got quiet then.

"Allright then, Al. Allright. Fine with me. But lemme ask you this…are you getting tired of me just being your sex partner, and is that what you're startin' to resent? We're both getting what we want, right?" I hesitated. She finally figured out the deal. "Well?" she asked. That made me mad.

"What do you think, Soma? I love you, girl, but I need more than just fucking. You're just too blind to see it."

"No I'm not. I know that you love me, but you have to realize that the relationship that we had just got too confusing. Plus, I think we were never the same once you went to college."

"Wow. So I guess my question now is, have or did you ever love me?"

"Yes, Al. You know I did, but as I said before, people tend to grow apart sometimes. I think how we're operating now is best, don't you think?"

"No, I don't. Soma, I…I gotta wanna bring closure to this situation."

"Which means what?"

"I think, and as much as it hurts…" my voice started to crack, "I just think we need to both go our separate ways, and just not bother each other anymore. For real this time."

After a long pause, she spoke again. "Is that what you really want?"

"No, it ain't want I really want, but I can't do this anymore. My feelings for you are here again, and that's just makin' it worse." She hesitated again. This time, a long, long pause. Then, "Okay," she sighed. "If that's what you want, I can't stop your decision. I just want you to come over so we can discuss it face to face." There she was, baiting me again.

"Soma, did you hear what I just said?" Tears started to well up on my face and run down my cheeks, but I fought to be strong. "I can't do this anymore. I don't wanna do this anymore. Please."

Soma didn't care. "I know. I know, Al, but I think that it would be best if we both said good-bye together face-to-face rather than just end it on the phone."

"Why?"

"Because the phone just makes things so cold and impersonal. I just wanna see you one last time. Please."

"No sex?"

"Nope."

"You sure?"

"I promise." She was lyin' her ass off.

I know that I was the fool for doing this, but reluctantly, I was like, "Sure."

"Cool! Be at my house about twelve–thirty next Thursday night."

"Twelve-thirty? Why so late? Sounds to me like another booty call."

"No, no. It'll just be quiet, 'cuz my folks'll be asleep, and that will give us a chance to really talk." Yeah, booty call.

"I don't know, Soma."

"Please, Al. I'm over here begging you on one knee. PLEASE."

After a long, long, LONG hesitation, I thought...

"Al?"

"Yeah."

"You still there?"

"Yeah, I'm still here."

"Well, what'cha gonna do?"

Pause. Then, "All right Soma, yeah. Yeah, I'll be there. But I'm warning you, this is absolutely the LAST TIME."

"Good, great, it's a date. See you next Thursday. Bye."

"Bye." I hung up the phone, and then my stomach started churning. I questioned myself, 'Can I do this? Do I really want to?' I thought about how much in the past I wanted to get back with her, how I begged and pleaded to her, then watched my feelings get dogged out by her. I thought about how suspicious and jealous I got over her seeing other guys...and then I thought about us being intimate. That's when I got a stiffy. Real stiff and hard. Hard as hell and horny as hell the more I thought about it. Shit, I hated it when the head below thought more than the head above. At that point, I was thinking with that one, and the feelings of my heart were being pushed back for the thinking of the one below.

I knew when I saw her again on next Thursday, we were gonna end up doin' it. Hell, I knew that when I set sights on her little sexy ass again, we were gonna do it. And believe me, I liked doin' it. At the same time though, I didn't wanna get hurt again, and I knew that once we did it, it was gonna be over. I knew that once this happened, even though it would be the last time, I would probably fall back in that rut of lusting after her and chasing the ghosts of what we used to be. But you know what, ya'll? No matter how many times you may wish, you can never go home again. Never. And I also knew and accepted that. I had to accept my fate; therefore I acknowledged fulfilling my destiny next Thursday night.

When Thursday night came, I was nervous as hell. I kept thinking to myself, 'Do I really want to do this? Can I really go through with it? Am I still gonna lust for her after this? What's going to happen after tonight? She said we weren't gonna do the nasty…yeah right.' As sexually hyper as we were, I knew that when I saw her, abstinence wasn't going to be in either of our vocabularies. I looked forward to seeing her, but at the same time, I didn't.

Eleven-thirty came around. By this time I was thinking about phoning her and calling the whole damn thing off. My stomach was hurting like hell, and my mouth started getting dry with my tongue getting thick in my head. My mode of thinking had switched from 'Can I do this' to 'I can't. It ain't right.' But then again, I started getting rock hard when I thought about our past. I dropped down to my knees and started to pray to build up my confidence.

"Lord," I began, "Please help a young brotha to be strong and break away clean from this situation. It's tough, Lord, and I'm know you know it. I also know that you are well aware about this situation, so I'm sure you know the pain I'm going through right about now. I also know that you know that I love her very much, but now I think it's strictly humpin' between us, and I don't wanna do this no more. I can't, 'cuz too much is at stake, and I don't wanna be used no more. So Lord, if you can, and by your will, please remove me from this situation and place me in a new one. I know that with you, anything is possible, so please, please, please help me, Father. In your precious name I pray. Thank you.' I rose up, and tears started to flow. Nevertheless, I began preparing myself. Little did I know that He heard me and was also gonna definitely move tonight.

Twelve-fifteen came and I was on my way. I felt strong, and in a strange kind of way, born again. I kept saying to myself, 'Must be strong. Must stay strong.' Twelve-thirty came, and I pulled up in her driveway, all the way up to the front door. Mistake Number One (you know I was young and stupid, to pull up to where her parents could look out the window and see my ride? Stooopid!) In retrospect, I should've pulled on the side of the street where the other cars were, but I wasn't thinking about that right now. At least I didn't pull up with the lights shining into the house, but still…

I walked around to the old rendezvous point (the sliding glass door). 'Gotta be strong. Gotta be strong. Gotta be…?

And then she appeared, wearing nothing but a skimpy little outfit. Damn! I went as weak as a limp dick with a 98-year-old woman to make love to. Show time.

She slid open the door. "Welcome," she whispered. "Come on in." I walked into the house.

"Hello," I said. She held out her arms. "Gimme a hug." Oh, but did I! I hugged her, and then her hand reached around to squeeze Best Friend. It was as if the dead returned to life.

"Mmmm," she purred. "Kinda glad to see me, huh?" as she took her hand off of him. I took her hand and put it back.

"I cannot tell a lie," I quipped, "Yes I am. And so is he."

"Oh yeah, I see that you are," as she continued to hold on to Best Friend for dear life.

"Soma, I believe that I agreed to come here tonight just to talk. That's what you said."

"Oh, okay," she said, loosening her grip. "I'm sorry." She sat down. I sat right next to her as she put her hand on my leg. "So let's talk," she said. I had to move her hand.

"Alright then," I said. "Soma, I came here tonight to tell you that basically it's over. I just can't keep on doing this. I need more."

Soma was as unsympathetic and horny. She heard me, but she wasn't listening. "I hear ya," she said. "But listen, we're makin' too much noise in here." We were in the den. "Let's move somewhere a little quieter, and then we can really talk." She took my hand and tried leading me into the guest bedroom. I stopped.

"Soma, you promised."

"I know. I just wanna get in here just to talk to you without no disturbances, y'know?"

"Just talkin'?"

"Yeah, just talkin'. I promise. Come on." She took my hand again, and we went on into the room.

Ya'll know what? Temptation is a mutha.

Especially when you're in the right place, but at the wrong time in your life. Think about it. Soma had on that sexy-ass outfit at twelve-thirty at night in the guest room at her parent's house, promising that all we were gonna do was talk. Sheeet. I don't know about you, but where I come from, that *seemed* like a perfect invitation to get busy! Do I look like I'm stupid? Hell naw!

We walked in and sat down on the bed. Now when you come in this room, the front of the bed is facing the wall, so if we were to get busy and someone were to walk in, they would see us way before we saw them. Damn, Soma was soooo tempting. But we HAD to talk.

"Soma," I began. "I've gotta tell you, this will be my last time seeing you, because I'm still in love with you, and this situation...well...I can't. I just can't. It's too much at stake."

"What's too much at stake?" she questioned. Like she didn't know! I hesitated. "Go on Al," she said softly.

"At the risk of sounding like a punk, I ain't gonna tell you, 'cuz you'll think I'm soft."

"No, baby…NO." She took my hand. "On the contrary. I told you to come here tonight, because I wanted to tell you.."

Oh Jesus, I thought to myself. My heart started beating real fast, my breathing got short, and my stomach started churning. What more damage could this girl do to me? She looked into my eyes and continued.

"I just wanted to tell you that I know that I've done you wrong for the longest time, doggin' you out, ever since you've been in college. But as I've said, it's all been because of my insecurities, and I know that I've done you wrong." I looked at her in amazement.

"So what're you sayin'?" I asked.

"I'm sayin' two things…no, actually three things. First of all, I'm sorry for doing these terrible things to you. Second, I know that you weren't being a punk. You know, when a man loves a woman, he REALLY loves a woman, especially when he cries over her, like you did with me, so I know for a fact that you love me. I just want you to know that your efforts didn't go unnoticed, nor were your tears disregarded. Deep in my heart, I know that you love me, and believe it or not, I still care for you. But sometimes we hurt the ones that we care about most, and it's really draining on the person who's putting forth the most effort. And sometimes in all this confusion is when we find that moment of clarity, and for some of us, that's when we realize that what we've been searching for has been here all along."

I shifted my position on the bed and asked her, "So in this moment of epiphany, exactly what are you sayin'?" That's when she just came with it and kissed me. Tongued me down hard. I didn't refuse it. This kiss lasted around five, six minutes tops. When she finished, I was like, "What was the purpose of that?"

"I did that to tell you that I've been thinking, and I really thought about it, and…I really want to get back with you. The more I tried to find greener grass, the more I came up trying to find my way back to my original pasture where I was comfortable. You, Al are my original pasture, the place where I never should've left. You know what I mean? Al? Al?"

I was in pure damn shock.

"Al, you understand what I'm sayin'? You can close your mouth now, baby." I couldn't do nothin' else, so I closed it.

"Al? Al? Can't you say something? Anything? " Somehow, I found the words to speak.

"Soma…I…I just don't know what to say. I am in total shock. Tell me this, though."

"What? Go ahead."

"What Godly event on this earth made you make this choice and change your mind?"

"I just felt that no one could do to me what you do."

"So in other words, no one could do this voodoo to you to the level that I do."

"Yes baby. I realize that it wasn't you…it was me. I tried to run away from my feelings, but my heart has always carried me back to you. I really do, and please believe me when I say it. I really DO love you, and I really wanna make it up to you by giving my all to you…starting tonight."

By this time, my head was reeling with emotion. I felt high as hell, as if I had smoked a pound of weed before she spoke to me, before I even came over. I was in shock, but at the same time confused, mildly happy and angry. Angry at her for playing this game with me. Angry at her for juggling my emotions. Angry at her for wasting time in order for her to realize what she wanted. Angry at myself for waiting for her subconsciously, hoping that she would have a change of heart and come back. And now that I had her in my palm, I didn't even want her.

She started to get undressed. "I just wanna make it right," she kept saying over and over.

"Soma, I just wanna say…" She kissed me again and this time put a finger to my lips. "Hush, don't talk now. Save it for later." She undressed me and spread her fine little body all over me, like hot syrup on hotcakes.
"Tonight is ours," she whispered and licked me in my ear. My ear is my Achilles' heel, so I went weak while Best Friend woke up.
"What you want me to do?" she whispered.
"Shit, anything you want to do," I gasped.

"Okay. I will," she whispered, and proceeded to kiss my chest, my arms, my neck, my stomach, my belly button, and then…she went downtown. Damn, temptation is a mutha.

This was a night that would stay with me forever. Not so much as what we were doing, but the aftermath. At first, it was all good. All damn good. We were going at it every way possible (again!), and it was turning out to be my own very private porn movie starring us. Looked like we were trying to break records. We were like rabbits, for God's sake. After she came that first time and then I got mine and we were laying there holding each other, we heard footsteps.

"Oh, shit," I whispered, "Your folks are up! What are we gonna do?"

"Al, just chill," she said, putting on her clothes and heading out of the room. She met her whoever it was at the front door.

"Soma…" It was her father. Oh shit, for real!

"Daddy?"

"Soma…why you coming out of the guest room?"

"Oh, Daddy, don't be silly. You know it's summertime, and heat rises. I'm in there, 'cuz it was crazy hot in my room."

"Hmph. I see." He motioned to the window and looked out.

"So…whose car is that out there?" She looked out the window.

"I don't know. It's a party across the street. Maybe that person decided to park in our driveway."

"It's a Celica, isn't it?"

"I don't know, maybe."

"Al has a Celica, doesn't he?" My heart started racing. "Yeah," said Soma, "But why would he be at the party across the street? You know we don't go together anymore, Daddy!"

He sighed. "Yeah, guess, I forgot." He closed the window curtain. "Damn folks at that party, parkin' their stinkin' cars over here," he muttered. "Didn't even invite us. Oh well. Looks like I'ma havta call a towing service to get it outta my driveway." Towing service?! Oh hell naw! Soma better tell his ass somethin' so I can get outta here. After he went back upstairs, she came back into the room.

"Guess you heard the news."

"Hell yeah, and that's why I'm fixin' to go."

"Wait…my dad won't be callin' that truck for awhile. I know this. So while you're still here…can we do it one more time?" I looked at her in disbelief.

"What? Are you insane? Do you hear yourself right now? And what about that lie you just told Richard?"

"What lie?"

"That lie saying that we don't go together other no more? What kinda shit is that?"

She took my face and held it in her hands. "Al, we just made new beginnings tonight. So you know I didn't mean what I told my dad. Chill."

She started undressing again. When she was buck-naked, she lay down on the bed and was like, "Come on. One more time. For me." I got harder than breaking out of Alcatraz. This time our session was intense, with me cumming so hard that my toes cracked, while she came back-to-back. Damn, ya'll, it was soo good. All positions, like it was the last time that we'd be together. Cowgirl. Reverse cowgirl. Missionary. Sideways. It was that adrenaline and that danger of being caught that intensified the situation. I felt that I could go one last time, 'cuz I didn't want this night to end, and Soma complied. Going for Round Three, we got into my favorite (and still favorite) position…doggy-style. I straight up dominated that ass. I made her bark like a dog, while slappin' that booty and making it jiggle.

"Yah, baby, yeah," I huffed. "Give me that thang, with your high yella fine-ass!" What'd I say that for? She started to throw it even harder. Almost threw me out of her.

"You like that, baby?" she huffed.

"Goddamn right! Just like that right there! Damn, you WORKING that thang! I'ma need you to bark for me again. BARK!"

She yipped. And yapped. We were so into it, we didn't even hear her daddy come back downstairs…and stop in the doorway of the bedroom…

"Ahem," as he cleared his throat.

Remember when I mentioned that when you entered into the bedroom, you could see the headboard against the wall, and the foot of the bed is near the door? When he walked in, my back was facing the door. So when he said "Ahem," we froze. Damn, I knew we should've done it on the side of the bed!

Before I knew it, he had come around one side of the bed and grabbed me by my neck, and had lifted me straight up out of Soma. She jumped out of the bed,

pleading to Raging Richard, "Daddy, no! I love him!"
He let go of my neck and cracked her across the face in
true pimp style, knocking her ass and the rest of her to
the floor.

"You lied to me!" he screamed. I wanted to do
something, but I couldn't. Sheeet, I wasn't gonna get my
ass kicked, butt-naked and all. I had to get my clothes
and get the fuck outta there. By this time, Soma had
gathered herself together and ran out of the room. Then
he turned back to me with the quickness.

"What the hell are you doing with my
daughter?" I had to have the smart mouth.
"What's it look like?" I shot back. The hell I
said that for? Raging Richard reached out and snatched
me by my neck again, lifted me up and drew back his
fist. I put up my hands like I was being held up.

"Hold it," I began. "If you hit me, you'd better
kill me, 'cuz if you don't, then we're gonna be rollin'..."
He hesitated, dropped his fist, and dropped me on the
ground.

By this time her mother, Killer Connie came in.
"What the fuck is goin' on down here?" she yelled.
Raging Richard was like, "Connie, just look!" She came
in the room and saw me standing there naked.

"What the?! Oh, my!! Mmmm!" She was
shocked, but could've been impressed.
"Connie!" Yeah, she was. She gathered herself.

"I mean... you get your clothes and get the hell outta here!"

"Where's Soma?" he asked me. I didn't respond. Soma was hiding out in the bathroom. He started walking in.

"Is she in here?" asked Richard. He knocked on the door. "Sure is!"

And with that, Killer Connie ran over to the bathroom, kicked the door in and slapped the shit out of Soma. Damn, two for two.

"I knew you were a whore! I just knew it!" she screamed at my girl. I could hear Soma pleading, "Mommy? Mommy?! No, Mommy, no! Aaaah!"

I knew at that point that Connie was kickin her ass somethin' awful. I tried to grab my clothes and run, but Rich saw me, and tripped me up in the hall.

"Just a damn minute! Where the hell do you think YOU'RE goin'? What's your damn phone number?"

"It's seven seven seven, nine three, eleven!" He grabbed the phone.

"Seven, seven...wait a minute! Isn't that a song?"

"You tell me."

"Oh, a wise-ass, huh?" He drew back his fist again, so I had to make my move. I yelled out, "Fuck you!" and rushed him in the hall, butt naked and all. I knocked him down, grabbed my clothes and ran out to my car. I jumped in, and peeled out. I was shaking like a leaf. ***This has got to be the worse night of my life***, I thought. Where could I go? I know that Soma ratted me out and gave them my number, but it's so late, and they're dealing with Soma and all. Still, I've got to calm the fuck down and tell someone. Then, I thought of my boy Sam who lived around the way from Soma. *That's* who I can talk to. I drove right over to the next street, up the ramp to his house, and started honking that horn like someone was trying to kill me. His dog was barking like crazy and was trying to break his chain to get to me, but by this time, please believe I did not give a damn. He came out in his drawers, yelling.

"Hey mu'fucka, what's your problem? Don't you know it's two thirty in the fuckin' mornin'?"

I rolled down the window. "Man, come here. I've got to tell you something. He came over to the window and then abruptly jumped back.

"Hey, fool! You know you ain't got no clothes on? The fuck is your problem?"

"Soma's folks caught us tonight." I'm still shaking. Sam's eyes got big.

"Caught ya'll doin' what?"

"Caught us in the mix."

"For real? Oh, shit!" He started cracking up. In the meantime, I was not amused.

"I don't think that's funny."

"Sheet, I do. I think it's funny as hell. You got caught fuckin' and now you out here butt naked. So whadda you want me to do?"

"Dude, I just came over here 'cuz I had to calm down. You know, get my shit together before I head home."

"So what happened to Soma?"

"Hell if I know. The last thing I heard was Connie kickin' the bathroom door in, and Soma cryin' out, 'Mommy! Mommy!', so I knocked Rich down, grabbed my clothes and got the fuck out." He just stared at me.

"What?" I asked.

"So you just left Soma there with her folks beatin' her ass?"

"Dammit Sam, what could I do? I mean really? I couldn't do shit! Rich had me by my throat, and when Connie came down, he forgot all about me. So that was my chance, and I bailed. I ain't goin' back, 'cuz Rich would probably try to fuck me up, knowhuti'msayin'?"

"Al, man, you went out like a bitch."

"Whatever. I'm just need to step out and put my clothes…"

"Oh hell naw. Put them shits on in the car!"

"Yeah, okay." I started putting on my clothes. Sam kept talking.

"You know you fucked up, right? What you need to do is hope that he ain't called your house yet!" Sam continued.

"Shit! I didn't even think about that! Got-Damn!" I started up the car again. "Man, lemme go, 'cuz she probably told him my real number!"

"You gave him a fake number?"

Young, Black, Talented, & Alone

"Seven seven seven, ninety three eleven."

"Like the song?"

"Yeah."

"Man, you stupid. Get the fuck outta here. And put some clothes on."

"Yup. Gone." I backed out the driveway and got the hell on.

The next day was the beginning of the weekend, and I was more jittery than a stripper who had to do a bachelor party all by her lonesome. I kept close to the phone, expecting it to ring, but it didn't. Saturday night, I didn't go NOWHERE. And then the phone rang about 9:30. I grabbed that shit like my life was gonna get pardoned by the governor.

"Hello?" There was a long pause.

"Hello?" I said again.

"You know that I will kill you."

"Who is this?"

"You know that I will destroy you." I recognized the voice.

"Mr. Trite...is that you?" He seemed shocked.

"What the?! How did you?" He hung up the phone fast as hell. Sunday afternoon he decided to call back. In his normal voice. And also with his ass on his shoulders, all cocky and stuff. I grabbed the phone.

"Hello?"

"Yes, this is Mr. Trite. Lemme speak with your mother."

"She's not here right now."

"Oh really? When will she be back?"

"To tell you the truth, Mr. Triton, I really can't answer that, because I don't know."

He hung the phone up in my face. My mom stepped into the room.

"Who're you tellin' I'm not here?"

I whipped around to face her. "What'chu talkin' about?"

"You just told someone I wasn't here."

"Naw, that was Marc askin' if Soma was over here."

"This early?"

"Well, he didn't know." The phone rang again. I jumped. "I'll get it!"

My mom just looked at me. "What's gotten into you? I'll answer it."

"But it's for…" Too late. I could hear the conversation.

"Hello? This is she. No, I've been here all this time. He did what?" Oh shit. "When was this? Well, I am so sorry about that. Let me apologize for his behavior. Oh, sure, when would you like to come by? Yes, today's fine. All right, see you then." She hung up the phone and glared at me. "What did I tell you about that little girl?"

"What?"

"Don't tell me 'what'. Didn't I tell you that that whole damn family was crazy and to stop messing with that girl?"

"But I love her."

"Don't sell that shit to me. You should have left her alone before they tried to hurt you."

"They almost did."

"And now, her daddy wants to come over and talk about what happened. I swear, you are always doin' **somethin'**!"

"Sorry."

"Yeah, you sure are sorry. You might as well get ready."

At seven thirty, he was there. My mom welcomed him in and he just stared at me. We all sat down in the living room. Him, my dad, my mom, and me. Soma was nowhere to be found. Raging Richard was breathing hard as hell and kept staring at me. My mom set it off first.

"So what happened, Mr. Trite?"

"Well," Richard began, stretching out his legs and crossing them, "Your son had my daughter, my own little daughter lying to me. Lying while looking at me dead in my face! On the night he was caught at my house, there was a party going on across the street, so I guess he thought that his car would blend right in by parking. I guess he didn't notice that there weren't any other cars parked in my driveway or on my side of the street."

"I guess not," my moms said.

"Dumb ass," my father chimed in. Whatever.

"Anyway," Richard continued, "When I first came down, Soma lied and told me that it wasn't Al's car parked in the driveway, and I believed her. And then…then I came downstairs again and *this* time caught your son with my daughter in a most uncompromising position. I had no choice but to act up and throw him out of my house, because he was wrong."

"Dead wrong," said my pops.

"And because he was wrong, I threw him out, since I have no jurisdiction to discipline him. However, I did discipline my daughter. It's my expectation for you to do the same for Al."

My mom was like, "So Mr. Trite, what is it specifically that you want me to do?"
I should've known what was coming.
"What I want is for your son to never see my daughter again for as long as he exists. Ever." I choked.
"Never again, huh?" my mom asked.
"That's right."

"Humph," my mom snorted. My dad didn't say a word. Richard just glared at her. Then after a long pause, he was like, "Is that all you can say?"with his legs crossing the other way.

"Well Mr. Trite, I'm just glad that he wasn't caught with a man. Otherwise, what happened happened. I really can't do or say anything to change it. To me, it looks like my son is not the villain here. Both of them were caught doing wrong, so it was just unfortunate that they were caught, and in your house. But as far as Al coming to see your daughter again, he won't be there again until he is grown, and maybe by that time, both of them can decide what they want."

"Well, I'm glad to know that," snorted Richard, both legs down and his face relaxing. "But, what Al did was damn near close to raping my daughter." Now, Richard knew that was a lie. I had to say something. I wasn't gonna let him fuck up my credibility with my folks.

"That's not true!" I shouted. "I love Soma!"

All the adults looked at me in disbelief. My dad shook his head. Then Richard spoke up.

"Love? What do YOU know about love?" he retorted.

"I know that I love her enough to go down with her. To the end," I shot back.

"See Mr. Triton," my mom started up again, "What you have to realize is that again, it was mutual consent, so both are responsible for what happened. It wasn't totally my son's fault. Your daughter plays a part in this too. If she hadn't willingly opened up your home and her legs, then you wouldn't be here preaching to us about my son the potential rapist. Plus I'm sure she wasn't hollering 'Stop!' when you caught them, now was she?" She looked over at me. "Al, do you have anything else to say?"

I looked over at Mr. Triton. "I just wanna say that to Mr. Trite that I'm sorry that you had to see what went on and caught us in the act, but realize that I love Soma, and I still want to see her and be with her. I realize I was wrong, but could you PLEASE find it in your heart to forgive both of us, and let me see her again, with you and your wife's consent, of course. PLEASE, sir." He smiled smugly. Then he stood up and got in my face.

"Not a chance in hell. And if you come by or if I even see your car in my neighborhood, I'm gonna try and blast ya. You understand me, son?"

"Yeah, I understand." All of a sudden, my mom stood up.

"All right, that's enough. Get out of my son's face." She walked towards the door. "I think it's time for you to go." Ma opened up the screen for him. "Now." He walked out, walked down the steps of the front porch, but stopped at the driveway. He turned around and stared at my mother.

"Suppose I don't want to leave?" he said through clenched teeth.

"Suppose I call the police and have you arrested for criminal trespassing?" she shot back, but was real cool with it

Long pause. Then, "Suppose I'm gone?" from his end.

"Yeah, how about supposing that?" my mom answered. He didn't say anything else, just turned and started walking up the driveway. Then he got to his car, got in, and got the hell on. My mom glared at me.

"Al," my mom started, "I don't ever want to see you with or calling that little girl again. You understand?" I just looked at her.

"Boy, don't look at me that way. DO WE UNDERSTAND EACH OTHER?" Reluctantly, I was like "Yeah, Ma. Yeah. I understand." We both turned and went back inside, and I went downstairs to my room and just cried. Cried my eyes and my heart out.

Now I know that society dictates how men should act; that they should be strong and stoic, and should face every situation head on with clenched teeth and drawn fist, but lemme tell you something, especially with the ladies…*EVERY* man cries, no matter how strong or macho we think we are. And I cried. Cried because of the fact that I'd fucked up royally. Cried because I thought that with all the trials and storms, she was the one, because of all the fire that we walked through. Cried because she was my first love, and lastly cried for the fact that no matter how much hurt and rage I had in me, I KNEW that as long as her daddy had anything to do with it, I would possibly never see Soma again. And at that time, that shit hurt, because she truly was my first love.

EPILOGUE

A couple of years have now gone by, and in those years, believe it or not, I have encountered Soma again. She's gone on with her life, gotten married, and has three little boys. I got married, and she crashed my wedding and reception, as well as come to visit my momma and me (when I still lived at home) during that time when her boys were babies, and told me all about her husband. She called me a couple of times after she visited me and sent holiday and birthday cards, but it just ain't the same.

This is my final thought about this. When I was with Soma, I thought that I was in love, and I'm sure she did too. But truthfully, didn't neither one of us know about love. Personally, I think that that word gets tossed around a lot and used very loosely. I think that for me, I was just captivated at the fact that someone who was cute and fine actually liked me, and I ran with it. I mean, look at how my description was in the Eighties: I was a walking fashion disaster. And to have somebody be kind to me in spite of...I had to take that chance and try. And it worked to a certain point.

For Soma, I think that she wasn't really looking for a relationship. From the description, she was cute and fine, so she really didn't have to go looking. Guys sniffed her out. But I think that for me, it was more compassion at first, because she didn't know me, but she saw that I was trying that night at the show. So she obliged me. And that compassion eventually turned into interest after me trying so hard to find out about her, and eventually, it led into a relationship. So we were both naïve. But showing interest on both parts? We both ate it up, being young and inexperienced. And look what happened in the end. Definitely a life lesson for both of us, I'm sure.

About the Author

Born at Crawford Long, raised down the street from Dixie Hills, and currently living on the outskirts of Atlanta, Nathan Alexander is a TRUE ATLien and "Gawgia Boy" to the bone. He attended Frederick Douglass High School (Doug High!), went to Morehouse College, and found his passion in education after other jobs didn't quite work out.. This passion has led to 25 years of helping, motivating, and inspiring students from all grade levels. As you can see, his passion includes writing, and writing vividly. He wrote Y.B.T.A. as a four part series in order to show how it feels when relationships start and end, beginning with his first book here. Nathan believes that this relationship is the determining factor of how guys form other relationships later on. But it is this one, the first love, that makes the most impact. In addition to writing, he enjoys producing music, deejaying, roller skating, drawing and painting, dancing, writing rhymes, meeting new people, working out, washing clothes and cooking. He currently resides in Fayetteville, GA.

www.ingramcontent.com/pod-product-compliance
Lightning Source LLC
Chambersburg PA
CBHW051929240626
47153CB00004B/1427